David Ralph Williams

By a lantern's light

ALSO BY DAVID RALPH WILLIAMS

GHOST STORIES

Olde Tudor
Dead Men's Eyes

ANTHOLOGIES

Icy creeps – gothic tales of terror

By a lantern's light

A Ghost Story

David Ralph Williams

LOXDALE PUBLISHING HOUSE

First published in 2019 by
LOXDALE PUBLISHING HOUSE

Original cover photography by Keith Hannant.

All other photographs used were created by the author.

*This book is dedicated to all loved ones who no longer walk
among us.*

David Ralph Williams

By a lantern's light

And still I hear, thy shores along,
All faintly ringing,
The notes of ghosts of birds that long
Have ceased their singing.

The River Maiden
Victor James Daley

One

W ilford Bailey approached the Portside Inn with his brown eyes as wide as pennies. The façade was gloomy, smothered by creeping ivy, and lacking in any recent and much needed restorations. To Wilford, the inn was a marvellous edifice. He set his large, cumbersome suitcase down on the brickwork path that ran along the side of the inn and removed his cap. His golden hair was caressed by the winds wistful hands as he stood and directed his gaze adoringly over every crumbling windowsill, piece of rotting woodwork, and fractured render.

The illustrated sign outside was held in a perpetual tilt, by the strengthening wind. It depicted a mariner's tricorn hat, superimposed over an anchor. There were many lamps hanging from iron hooks outside, some of them were lit and had thus far managed to endure the wind's gusts. Picking up his heavy suitcase, he made his way over to the doorway and entered the inn.

Inside, it was a stark contrast to the temperature outdoors. There was a well-fed open fire that warmed the large interior and produced an agreeable aroma. Wilford carried his case and set it down near the foot of the bar. The room was filled with twenty or more patrons; the majority were men. Most of the people inside the Inn were engaged in strident conversation.

Wilford tipped his cap towards two men close to him at the bar, both reciprocated with a similar gesture. One of them was busy stuffing tobacco into a long walnut pipe that he had clamped between his molars. He offered Wilford his tobacco tin, but not being a pipe smoker or any smoker for that matter he declined politely.

"Excuse me, but would either of you know where I may find the landlord of the inn?" Wilford asked. The man who had now finished loading and lighting his pipe pointed towards a large brass bell fixed to the upper tankard rack on the bar. There was a rope hanging from its clapper. Next to the bell was a hand-written sign that read, *'Ring for attention.'* Wilford thanked the pipe smoker and he gave the rope a gentle tug.

"Not like that," said the man who then yanked the rope boisterously from side to side producing a fearsome *CLANGING*. Wilford now felt terribly embarrassed as all eyes were now on him and conversation halted momentarily only to slowly resume.

A moment later a tall burley man, the innkeeper, emerged from a door behind the bar. He had oily lank hair with a fringe that reminded Wilford of the type worn by Oliver Hardy. His face was craggy and unshaven, yet he wore a pristine navy-blue waistcoat and crisp white stiff collared shirt. The smoking man removed the pipe from his lips to point at Wilford. The innkeeper then approached him.

"You rang bell?" he said simply. He looked a little annoyed and Wilford now felt even more ashamed even though he had not actually rung the bell so loudly himself. He offered his hand in a friendly gesture and the innkeeper took it,

"Yes, sorry about that. My name's Wilford Bailey. I booked a room here, for four weeks." The innkeeper glanced at the bell, then back at Wilford,

"Four weeks you say?"

"Yes, that's right. You were expecting me? I am at the right place?" The innkeeper nodded.

"Aye, you're the chap from Oxford?"

"Yes indeed, the very same," replied Wilford cheerily. "And may I say it, what a delightful place."

"I like to think so, thank you sir. Pardon me sir, my name's Burt, Burt Prescott," Wilford gave Burt's hand another quick shake,

"How'd you do," he said. Burt lifted the serving hatch and came through from behind the bar.

"This your case sir?" he asked as he picked it up, seemingly as though it was empty.

"Ah, yes. Just the one," added Wilford.

"Aye, a big un at that." Burt said as he walked past Wilford and beckoned for him to follow. "I'll show you to your room."

When the door to the room was opened, Wilford entered followed by Burt who set his suitcase down for him on the bed. Burt walked over to the single window and pointed outside. "Nice views, of the waterways from up here." Wilford joined him and peered out. The night was almost in, but he could make out the rippling moonlight as it danced upon the currents that were being tirelessly licked by the squalls outside. He saw many narrowboats moored near the banks on which the Portside Inn stood, their small black chimneys puffed out black smoke that was whisked away on the wind's breath. "You asked for a desk. I hope this will do." Said Burt as he wiped a hand across the small yet sturdy oak furniture under the window.

"It will do perfectly. Thank you," said Wilford.

"Will you be wanting supper sir?"

"Supper would be very much welcomed. I'm famished after such a long journey from Oxford," replied Wilford rubbing his hands together at the prospect of a warm meal on such a stormy night.

"Thing is sir, my wife usually does all the cooking, but she's feeling a bit under the weather, so you will have to make do with my efforts. Mutton stew is what we got tonight sir."

"Mutton stew sounds delicious, and I hope your better half makes a speedy recovery."

"Thank you, sir, Mrs Prescott is usually in fine fettle, never so much as a cold. She says it's the change sir, if you know my meaning."

"Indeed I do, but please convey to her my best wishes would you." Wilford removed his overcoat and placed it around the chair that faced the desk. Burt added that supper will be ready in about an hour before leaving Wilford alone in his room.

Wilford unfastened his suitcase and removed another smaller, heavy box from within. His clothes had filled the remaining spaces around the smaller box. He set the box down on the desk and unclipped two clasps on the front that secured the lid. The lid was unfurled to reveal a glossy, ivory and red Princess 300 portable typewriter. The underside of the lid contained a slot holding at least 100 sheets of virgin white paper.

Wilford removed a single sheet of paper and fed it into his typewriter so that it was ready for when he chose to begin working. He laid out his toiletries neatly on a dresser next to a tall dark-veneered wardrobe in which he placed the few shirts, two jackets, and two pairs of trousers that he'd brought with him. He placed a few items of underclothing inside a drawer at the base of the wardrobe. When he had finished unpacking, he kicked off his shoes and stretched out on the bed with his hands behind his head. He thought he'd try and get a few minutes of rest before going down for supper.

Wilford Bailey was thirty-four years old and unmarried. He had not been enlisted during the war when he had turned eighteen because he had been born with only one lung, his right. According to his doctor, a person may live a normal life and having only one lung doesn't necessarily affect life expectancy. He discovered early on that he was not able to exercise as strenuously or for as long as a person with two lungs.

Instead of fighting during the last years of the war, Wilford helped the war effort building Spitfires, mainly at Castle Bromwich and Southampton. After the war he began his studies at Oxford reading politics and history.

Wilford made a living from writing books about the supernatural. He didn't write fiction as such, instead he was a chronicler of historical accounts passed mouth to mouth prior to being written down. He had so far written and published two books, the second of which had given him some degree of success as a professional writer.

His first book was a compilation of ghostly tales collected from various family archives that had been preserved for posterity. The accounts he had amassed concerned the aristocracy of the Victorian era, whose grandiose houses laid claim to all manner of preternatural shenanigans. Wilford managed to find a publisher for his book whilst he continued his studies at Oxford.

The book had some success, enough for him to think seriously about his once chosen career path in journalism.

His second book appeared some three years after the first. This book concentrated mainly on ghost sightings and theories during the present times, notably since the end of the war leading up to the beginning of the 1950s. The second book was even more successful than the first, in fact, his first book enjoyed a further print run and his publisher was very anxious that Wilford should immediately begin work on a third. Now living off the proceeds of his first two books, Wilford had quit his day job at the Illustrated London

News so that he could concentrate solely on his new unconventional writing career.

It was whilst spending some time at Oxford University library, in the archive section, that Wilford stumbled across an old newspaper article that highlighted tales of ghosts around Britain's waterways. The Wormbridge waterway near Ulverstone, Cheshire, was noted as possessing such an unnerving track history with respect to ghosts and ghouls. The article listed some accounts as relayed by visitors to the area as well as by some of the local population who at the time the article was written, worked on the waterways themselves.

The whole idea of haunted rivers and canals was enough to inspire Wilford to use these settings for the subject of his next book. Immediately he began to collect and collate as many accounts from around the country. He had spent the last six months travelling the canals on chartered boats, mostly small cruisers and tug-trawlers, and the occasional narrowboat. He had become quite the boatman. With nearly all the material collected for his third book, he wanted to save the Ulverstone waterways till last.

Although Wilford wrote about ghosts, he didn't believe in them. He left all those fanciful leanings to his readership. His job, as he saw it, was to merely provide the basic facts and the witness statements, embellished of course with a poetic flair; however, just enough to capture the imagination of his readers. If anything, life and experience had taught him that a tangible explanation was never far from the truth when presented with tales of a supernatural kind.

It was the waterways near Ulverstone that seemed to have the most solid and authentic stories than other riverways upon which he had recently travelled. The original article he had found and copied precisely into his notebook listed all the accounts and witness statements relating to the ghost of a waterside spectre known locally as *Aggie*.

There were two distinct stories regarding *Aggie*: one story claimed that *Aggie* was the victim of a drunken boatman who assaulted her and then drowned her in the canal at Wormbridge, just where the old bridge used to stand. The other story, being even more nefarious, concerns the murder of a child by the father, a local lockkeeper. *Aggie*, the mother of the aforesaid child, is reported as being seen wandering the waterways searching for her lost daughter.

Back in the days when Ulverstone was a working canal system, shipping coal to the rapidly industrialised cities of the northwest, there were many reported cases of a phantom who it was said had the power to overturn a boat. By means unreported, this phantom could prevent the crew from escaping a watery grave. Whether or not this was at the hand of *Aggie*, and why she would want to do such a thing was something that Wilford intended to investigate. He always took it upon himself to unravel the often, *muddled* tales, and to tie them together with a more satisfying sense of logic. He was in fact creating new folklore out of the old parables.

***

Wilford had managed to catch at least twenty or so minutes of sleep before he came down for supper. The inn was full. The fire crackled noisily in the brickwork grate as men and women enjoyed glasses of ale and sweet wine. There were not many tables, and the few that were placed about the dining room were mostly taken except for two. He eyed both tables, but none of them really appealed to him. One was jammed right up against a somewhat dirty looking brick wall, and the other seemed to face the lavatories. After choosing the best of two bad worlds, he opted for the small table that butted up to the brick wall.

There was a single folded piece of paper on the table. Once he had sat himself down, he unfolded it and read what would have been the night's menu. His mouth watered at the prospect of smoked haddock pie, beef stew and dumplings, cottage pie, or a mixed grill. Everything had been crossed out and '*Mutton stew*' had been pencilled in at the top. At least he didn't have to make any choices he thought to himself as Burt approached his table. "Evening sir," said Burt, "are you still wanting supper?"

"I would like some of the mutton stew if you have any left," spoke Wilford.

"Aye, plenty left sir. I will bring you some over. Would you like a drink fetching too?"

"Yes, I am rather thirsty. A pint of your best ale would be nice." Burt placed some cutlery down onto a napkin.

"Right you are then sir, shan't be long," he said as he made his way through the bar and back-of-house.

Wilford pulled out his notebook that he always carried. It was a stout and sturdy little book, leather bound, and it had a narrow pocket in the spine where he kept a small pencil. He began making notes, describing the Inn and the clientele within. Before he had travelled to Ulverstone, he had studied a map of the area. The Portside Inn was situated at a place where the waterways converged. He figured that local people from all over would drop by, mooring their vessels whilst they ate and drank. In time, he would initiate conversation with the locals, to see what interesting tales they might have about the so-called phantom of Wormbridge.

Burt returned with Wilford's dish of mutton stew, bringing him a tankard of dark ale and a wedge of sourdough bread. The stew was surprisingly flavoursome, and the ale malty and textured. As he sat enjoying his solitary meal, he caught sight of another lone diner, a woman.

She sat at a small table illuminated by a single candle in a glass bowl. She wore a blue, slim, sheath dress and had a matching blue knitted shawl around her shoulders. She had glossy chestnut hair, perfectly curled and coiffed. She had her back to him; Wilford wondered and imagined how she'd look should she glance in his direction.

For a fleeting moment, she turned and scanned the room. Her eyes and Wilford's met just for a second, and in that instant, he thought that he'd never seen anybody so beautiful. He watched as she searched for something or someone. He assumed that she must be looking for her husband, or dinner date, because someone so beautiful and charming couldn't possibly be alone.

Suddenly she smiled a dazzling smile as Burt made a line for her table and then he proceeded to clear away the empty supper dish and cutlery. Maybe she was alone, thought Wilford, and after his second tankard of ale he decided he now had enough Dutch courage to be bold enough to introduce himself.

18

As he walked over towards her, he thought of a million reasons why he shouldn't be doing what he was about to do. What would she say? Would she simply dismiss his attempt to meet her with a courteous yet killer jibe? He remembered the last time he had randomly introduced himself at a dance in Croydon when he was feeling full of beans celebrating his first ever pay cheque. He had spotted Sally, a secretary during his time working at the Illustrated London News. He had asked Sally if she would like to dance. Sally, without looking at him simply said: *'You know I always say there's no such thing as stupid questions. Just stupid people.'* Wilford, slightly crestfallen, apologised before sloping away to stand at the bar.

"Hello, please forgive this intrusion, but I wondered if I may join you at your table?" spoke Wilford. "I'm dining here alone, and it looks as though you might also be similarly fixed. It's such a gloomy old place and maybe we could both cheer each other up somewhat?" Wilford waited for her to respond; graciously she offered the empty seat to Wilford who sat down then offered his hand. "Wilford Bailey," he introduced himself with a smile.

"Corinne," she replied taking up the offer of Wilford's handshake.

"I hope you don't mind me intruding on your evening, it's just that-"

"Oh no, you're not intruding." Corinne. said. "Truth is, I was rather bored and was about to go to bed. I was looking forward to taking a bath before I do." Wilford noticed her fingernails matched her bright red lips.

"Oh, I'm sorry. Look, if you'd prefer to be alone, I can go to my own room. I have a book I'd like to get started on." Wilford said, realising he had probably imposed on this poor woman more than he should have.

"Oh, you like reading? What is your book about Mr Bailey?" she asked him. Even though they had only met mere seconds ago he found that he felt quite easy in her company. He hoped that Corinne felt the same. He saw that she appeared to study his neat Teutonic hair, and noticed how her cheeks sometimes flushed red as she listened to what he was saying.

"Well, it's a book I will start to write, you see that's why I'm here," he said.

"A book you are writing? How interesting! So, you are an author Mr Bailey?"

"Please, call me Wilford, or Wilf. Much friendlier don't you think?"

"But I hardly know you Mr Bailey."

"That is true, but now we have introduced ourselves to one another, we are no longer strangers, don't you see?" said Wilford playfully.

"What kind of books do you write Wilford?" Asked Corinne. Now he had to decide. Did he tell her the truth, that he wrote about ghosts and run the risk of completely alienating himself and possibly face ridicule? Or, should he could tell his usual white lie and claim to be a writer of local history and folklore. The glint in Corinne's almost cerulean blue eyes told him that he need not fear speaking the truth this time.

"I write about ghosts," he said earnestly.

"Ghosts?"

"Yes, I know how that sounds believe me. But please don't think of me as a fool."

"Wilford I would never see you as a fool. I think one must be very clever to write a book, don't you agree? Whatever the subject."

"Well, I'm not sure I would have the audacity to describe myself as clever. Writing isn't something they can teach you at school, it's something you're born with, something you learn to do. Writing kind of comes from within you. Oh, of course you can learn to read and write, you can learn about grammar, and to some degree school can give you the foundation of basic worldly knowledge. But, the stories, the descriptions, the observations, they come from your own personal experiences."

"Ghosts—how do you write about ghosts? I mean, you must believe in them to write about them, wouldn't you say? What do ghosts mean to you?" Corinne asked, and she sat back in her seat, waiting for his reply. Wilford thought a moment before answering.

"A ghost can mean a lot of things. It can mean the feeling of longing for something, or a place. It can be the memory associated with an old injury, or a traumatic experience. A ghost can be a mere shadow, or hint of something. You see, it doesn't always have to be a creaky staircase on a stormy night, or the spirit of a drowned child." Corinne's expression changed, she looked saddened by Wilford's last words.

"Why did you say that? About a child?"

"Well, one of the reasons I'm here is to look into the account of the Wormbridge ghost. Have you heard of it?"

"I can't say that I have. Please tell me of it." Corinne asked. Wilford folded his arms, Burt was hovering around their table. He waited for him to be far enough away, just out of earshot before he continued to speak.

"Legend has it, that around these parts the spectre of a woman is rumoured to be responsible for the sinking of many boats over the years. It is believed that she is looking for her dead daughter who drowned in the canals, or rivers nearby. The story is a little ambiguous, but I hope to get to the bottom of it and wrap up the facts as far as they can be made out."

"What an interesting story, but are you sure you should be poking around with such a sensitive local topic? I mean, what if the locals become, umm, upset?"

"Well Corinne, I aim to be tactful and sensitive. I will use my amiable charms." He followed with a smile. Corinne countered with one of her own. "But you haven't told me what you are doing here, in Ulverstone," he probed. Corinne placed her elbows on the table and leaned into Wilford slightly.

"I'm looking for a place to live. I have a lot of family history here, but I just haven't found the right place yet."

"I see, so you are staying here, at the inn indefinitely?"

"That's the plan, for now. Until I find what I'm looking for."

"That must cost quite a lot of money Corinne, unless Burt has special rates for long-staying guests. Do you mind if I ask what you do for a job?"

"Should I give up all my secrets at once. Can I not retain some air of mystique?" Said Corinne friskily. Wilford smiled, and chuckled,

"Of course, you don't have to tell me anything," he said. Corinne glanced at a large wooden wall mounted clock.

"Well, it has been very pleasant chatting to you Wilford, but I am feeling tired and would rather like to have that warm bath I spoke of earlier." Wilford nodded, and he rose from his seat as Corinne stood up.

"Perhaps we could get together again soon, maybe we could meet for dinner, if you'd like to?" he said hopefully.

"Yes, I'd like that. But please be careful Wilford. These locals can be a little suspicious and defensive. Especially with strangers." Corinne said goodbye and she walked out of the dining room leaving Wilford pondering about her advice and about her in general.

***

The next morning, after a good sleep, Wilford set out early. He had left the inn and walked a mile or so along the canal towpath to the boatyard where he was to collect his hire boat. The walk was a pleasant one, the wind had died almost to a complete stop, a stark contrast to the previous day's tempestuous evening.

There was already a vast amount of steam fog rising from the sunlit water, creating a vaporous soup close to the surface. A pair of ducks cut a line along the centre of the canal, through the haze, occasionally stopping to feed on strands of surface weed. Wilford thought just how much of a lonely place this was. Other than the occasional passing narrowboat or barge, his walk was almost one of solitude.

Gone was the hustle and bustle of only a few years since, when waterways such as this acted as highways for the transport of all manner of fuel and commodities. It was hard for Wilford to imagine such a scene now. The type he had witnessed as a boy or even a younger man. The kind of business that used the waterways had shifted to roads and rail. The transporting of goods by road was much faster; more cost effective. A shift from traditional industries had also accelerated the decline of the waterway system.

Wilford pondered as he walked if he should eventually bear witness to the final death throes of these canals, especially with the promise of a network of motorways. Macmillan had won a landslide victory in the general election. Wilford believed Macmillan won because of the construction of the new motorway, and with the help of daily newspapers capturing the public's excitement calling the motorway a *'Space age highway.'* It seemed the future method of hauling had been decided.

The low sunlight glinted off the shiny painted signage that read *'Rose and Castle narrowboats for hire.'* Wilford walked past an assortment of vessels all tethered in lines of four; however, carefully butted up against each neighbouring boat's rope fenders. There were various types of boats for hire, and Wilford's recently acquired boating experiences had given him new knowledge about which was best suited for his own personal needs.

He surveyed the lines of cruisers, narrowboats and barges. The last time he had hired a boat was back in the summer. During that occasion, he opted for a small cruiser style, with a cabin, but little else. The warm summer had dispelled the need for anything more insulating. This time however, due to the seasonably damp and cool weather of mid-November, he had decided to charter a traditional narrowboat and was looking for one with some internal homely comforts.

As Wilford stood imagining which of the boats he could see himself steering along the canals and rivers, he was set upon by a black Labrador who came joyfully over to greet him. The dog wagged its tail happily as Wilford gave it a gentle fuss about the ears. "Jess, Jess, come on now girl, leave the man alone." Came a scolding voice from behind. Wilford turned and saw a short stocky man wearing a bowler hat and a thick duffle coat walking in his direction. "Jess, I've told you once, don't mither the man." The man in the bowler and duffel smiled at Wilford, "Sorry sir, excuse my dog," he said apologetically, "she won't bite, she's just overfriendly," the man explained. Wilford continued to fuss the dog,

"No need to apologise, she reminds me of my old dog. Why, they could have been two peas in a pod!" said Wilford happily. The Man in the duffel introduced himself as Howard Durnsten, owner of the boatyard. He asked Wilford if he'd come about a boat.

"Yes, I have. You might remember? I made a call at the end of last week. I was looking to hire a narrowboat, a boat with all the creature comforts so to speak," explained Wilford. Durnsten nodded,

"Oh yes I remember, I have him ready sir, if you'll follow me." Howard said and gestured for Wilford to accompany him.

"Him? Aren't boats and ships usually referred to in the female gender?" spoke Wilford as he and Durnsten walked past a cluster of trussed boats toward a single boat, tethered simply to a mooring ring on the bank.

"Aye, normally, but this one's name stops me from calling it a she." Durnsten pointed to a brightly painted predominantly red, narrowboat. The name *'Knotty Buoy'* was inscribed using intricate black script along the side. "He was built back in 1930, almost thirty years old. A fine boat sir, not so owd and feggy," added Durnsten proudly, meaning that the boat was not so old and in good condition. Wilford also nodded agreeing with Durnsten: the boat was indeed a fine-looking craft.

"He's about forty-feet by almost seven-feet. There's a double birth under the tug deck, with a single bunk further down." Durnsten beckoned for Wilford to follow him on deck. Both men climbed onto the wall deck and went into the cabin through a hatch under the cratch cover.

Inside, Durnsten pointed out the boats features, "This large bed," he said referring to the one built under the front end, beneath the tug deck, "it's nice and roomy, but I'd use the single bunk further down, as that one's near the stove. It can get quite chilly in the colder months, in a boat like this. Sleeping further down will make things more bearable."

"To be honest, I'm not planning on spending the night on the boat," said Wilford, "I have a room at the Portside Inn. I shall be cruising mostly by day."

"Very wise sir, like I said, the nights are beginning to get a lot colder, but even in the day, sitting below decks, the water's cold and you'll find yourself needing the stove sir. I've left some kindling and some coal in a waterproof box on the deck. There's a scuttle near the stove which is already filled."

Durnsten took him further down the boat. He pointed out the fresh water tank, seating, and living quarters, all of which were decorated by scumbling and traditional roses and castles. He demonstrated the electric cabin lighting explaining that although electric lights were fitted, to reduce power consumption the boat had retained some original oil lamps fixed to the walls between the porthole windows.

He then showed him the engine fitted in the rear cabin. "It's got a Lister engine, used to be a hand-start but was converted to electric start by my late uncle, he was a retired Lister engineer," explained Durnsten. Wilford nodded, he was familiar with both types of engines. "There's a full tank of diesel sir, should keep you going for the duration I should think."

"Do I have sufficient mooring ropes, steaks, or an anchor?"

"You do sir! If you'll follow me up on deck, I will show you."

Durnsten indicated where the mooring ropes were kept, along with steaks and mallets. The anchor was positioned at the stern, and he demonstrated to Wilford how it should be operated. Durnsten now turned Wilford's attention towards a large polished brass tunnel lamp, mounted on the roof at the front. "This is your headlamp, there's also a second lamp fitted at the rear stern. I put new bulbs in last week, so both should be good for many hours. You'll need it as this time of year the fog's thick as eels in jam, and driving through tunnels, especially the ones round these canals can be a nerve-racking experience because of how lengthy they are."

As Wilford and Durnsten continued to go through some other details on the boat, heavy fat raindrops began to dimple the surface of the water. Soon the rain began to splatter on the deck as the sudden emerging cascade grew heavy.

"It's tipping down," said Durnsten, the brim of his bowler beginning to drizzle rainwater onto his shoes. "Shall we go inside the boathouse to finish off all the particulars?" Wilford agreed, and they jumped onto the bank and made haste towards a white rendered square building with a smoking chimney.

Inside the boat house, Wilford and Durnsten were busy signing the leasing documentation that released *Knotty Buoy* to Wilford. A warm fire skipped merrily in the grate and Mrs Durnsten brought in a teapot sporting a bright knitted cosy. She poured them both a cup of hot brew before adding some more coal to the fire. Jess sat and dried her wet fur in front of the fire.

The rain began to hammer on the windows of the boathouse, "My, what a lot of fuss the weather makes today," said Mrs Durnsten as she turned on another lamp in the room. The dark clouds outside were grasping onto what little sunlight the day provided. Howard Durnsten lit himself a cigarette and offered his cigarette case to Wilford. Wilford declined,

"It's a little unusual to take a holiday on the waterways this time of year, if you don't mind me saying sir," spoke Durnsten as he puffed on his cigarette. Wilford handed back the papers he had signed to Durnsten.

"It's more of a working holiday you see,"

"Working ... oh."

"Yes, you see I am a writer by profession, and I am here to finish my latest work," explained Wilford.

"A writer? Bless my soul! We don't have many writers hire our boats, do we my dear?" said Howard. Mrs Durnsten shook her head,

"Good gracious no! Mostly fishermen, or those who like to watch the birdlife. But not this time of year," Howard's better half replied.

"You write books about boating? Is that it?" Durnsten continued to probe.

"Not really, although boats do feature a lot in my current book. I am involved in a project regarding the local history of Ulverstone, and especially its folk tales, the traditional stories if you know what I mean," explained Wilford. Durnsten scratched his head then turned to look at his wife who was already giving her husband a discerning stare.

"Not sure as I do sir. Do people buy books about other folk's local stories?" asked Durnsten dubiously.

"Yes, it's becoming very popular. And I must say, there are many fine stories around these parts are there not?" Mrs Durnsten began shifting uneasily in her chair, she lent down and stroked Jess who lolled onto her side providing access to her under-belly for her to rub. Howard Durnsten looked similarly anxious. Wilford continued, "I was hoping you'd be able to tell me a place where I might be able to talk to some local boaters; collect some of their shaggy-dog tales if you like."

"Well sir, there's the old Otter, a nice traditional public house about a couple of miles out along the cut," Durnsten pointed out of a rain-washed window indicating the direction to take. "It has good moorings, and good food to boot."

"Thank you, I will make that my first port of call," said Wilford happily.

"I must warn you though, the locals are not so eager to talk to outsiders, they can be tight lipped at the best of times and I hasten to say, a little aloof," warned Durnsten before taking Wilford by surprise and asking him for a deposit on the boat, in case of damages.

"You never mentioned this before," said Wilford as he took out his cheque book. "How much is the deposit?"

"I think a hundred and fifty pounds should cover it. Sorry to spring this upon you sir, I must have forgotten to mention it when you called. You will have it back sir, once the boat is returned."

"I haven't been asked for a deposit when hiring boats before," said Wilford slightly surprised. He had enough in his bank

32

account to cover this apparent formality, so it wasn't much of a concern. He handed Durnsten the signed cheque.

"Thank you, sir, like I said, this will be returned to you once *Knotty Buoy* is brought home safe and sound. It's just that these waterways are not without some risk," Durnsten said without further elaboration.

Durnsten led Wilford back outside once the rain had died down. He helped him untie the moorings on *Knotty Buoy*. Wilford hopped on deck and used a mooring pole to push the boat away from the bank, "It's a bit shallow at the border sir, I would push him out before starting the engine fully, otherwise the prop will plough up the bottom!" shouted Durnsten. Wilford nodded and kept the engine in neutral until he was away from the bank. Happy he was in sufficient depth, he started the engine.

The pleasing chugging sound gave him comfort as he took hold of the steering rod attached to the rudder. *Knotty Buoy* glided through the cut and Wilford turned to give Durnsten a departing wave who responded similarly before turning back to the boathouse.

Standing on the stern, holding the steering rod, Wilford's hands were becoming numb with the chilly air. He wished that he had packed a pair of gloves and intended to buy some at the first opportunity. After cruising for just under half an hour he passed a sign on the bank advertising the Otter public house. The sign indicated that the Otter was only about five hundred yards in front, just through a short tunnel ahead.

Wilford slowed the boat down and turned on his headlamp. He could see the tunnel was one-way; there were no other boats on the opposite approach, so he continued through keeping the boat at the centre. Once through the tunnel he saw the Otter set back from the bank, and as Durnsten had said, the moorings were more than adequate.

Wilford glided *Knotty Buoy* slowly, pointing the front end towards the bank. He set the boat in reverse just as the bow bumped off its rope fenders. With the engine now in neutral he waited for the boat to come in line close to the bank. When he was happy, he switched off the engine and jumped off the deck holding the bow mooring rope. He fastened the rope securely to a mooring post before tying up the stern. Happy with his handiwork, he climbed the short grassy hill to the path leading to the Otter.

Before he entered the public house, Wilford scanned the boats all moored on the far side of the bank. He counted eight in total and noticed that they each had a figurine or maybe a child's doll secured to their fenders. Rubbing his cold hands together, he stepped inside.

As a stark contrast to the Portside Inn, this place was almost noiseless other than the ticking and chiming of an old grandfather clock standing in a recess beside a large inglenook fireplace. There were a few groups of boaters huddled about tables set out in the main bar room. The bar itself was propped up by a few men who smoked and took occasional gulps from ale mugs as they chatted in low inobtrusive voices.

At the bar, Wilford read from a menu board that had various bar meals written in white chalk. He ordered himself a mug of Ridlington ale and a plate of lamb's liver, mash potato and gravy. He turned and scrutinised the clusters of boaters, choosing the table he would eventually intrude upon, where he would aim to get a conversation started about the stories of the Wormbridge ghost.

The table he chose was near to the fire. There were three people seated at the table, two men and a woman. Both men wore what Wilford assumed to be the traditional boater's apparel, neckerchiefs, waistcoats and collarless shirts, with army surplus thick woollen overcoats on top. The woman wore a thick cheesecloth dress with a heavy shawl, her hair was hidden beneath a boatwoman's bonnet.

Wilford's meal and ale was placed onto the bar and he carried it over to the trio seated at the table. He used the excuse that he needed warmth from the fire following a stint on the canals and they all made room for him, even fetching him an unoccupied seat from a facing table.

After some introductions and small talk about the state of the waterways and whether or not the winter would be as bad as that which occurred a few years back in forty-seven, Wilford now finished with his meal bought everyone at the table a drink from the bar. With everyone happily sipping their drinks Wilford took the plunge and revealed that he was travelling the area collecting supernatural stories and yarns relating to Wormbridge's ghost.

The first of his new acquaintances, Fred Bulby, scoffed at the local myths surrounding Ulverstone, in particular, the ghost of *Aggie*.

"If you ask me, man who believes in all that twaddle needs to give his 'ead a wobble. Must have bad luck top end," said Fred pointing at his own crown. This ignited a bout of laughter chiefly from himself.

"I take it you don't believe in the stories then," asked Wilford taking out his notebook from an inside pocket of his coat.

"No, I do not. But this 'ere dogwallop does, don't he!" chuckled Fred pointing at the other man who had introduced himself and his wife as Jim and betty Hughes. Wilford turned his attention onto Jim and Betty.

"Fred says you believe in the stories, is that right?" Jim looked sheepish at Fred before speaking.

"Aye, I right do! But I have reason to. See, I saw it once I did, not that no one believes me, 'sides Betty," answered Jim.

"So, when did you see her, the ghost I mean?" asked Wilford, whose pencil was poised over a clean page in his notebook.

"Not sure it was a her though. Orrible it looked, reet 'orrible!"

"Oh you daft bugger, arseholed and three sheets to the wind you was no doubt," scoffed Fred, who was quickly corrected by Betty.

"No 'im weren't, he was only a nipper," she said in Jim's defence.

"Aye, that's right. Ten-year-old I was," added Jim.

"Ten-year-old and wi' a 'ead full of slutch or mud," laughed Fred as he slurped at his ale. He excused himself after belching loudly.

"Don't listen to what he says," shouted Betty, "go on, tell the man what you saw Jim."

Two

J im Hughes, or little Jimmy, as he was known back then was ten years old when his dad gave him his first fishing rod. Jimmy had come home from school on a Friday, and when he'd finished his supper, his dad winked at him and told him that when he was done washing up the supper pots and plates for his ma, he should come out back to the shed, because he had something to give him.

Jimmy washed up quickly, partly because of the surprise promised by his father, and partly because the water was almost scolding hot. His ma had boiled the water on a large pot on the kitchen stove before tipping it into the cast iron sink. Jimmy scrubbed up the plates and pots and placed then neatly on the side to drain. His dad came in and saw that he had finished. With a newly lit pipe hanging from his lip, he slipped on his boater's jacket and told Jimmy to follow him outside.

Jimmy loved being invited to his dad's shed. It was a place of wonder, full of tools many of which he hadn't the faintest idea what they were used for. There were other curious bits and pieces of old boats, propellers, rudders, and lots of rope. Jimmy's dad earned his living working as a canal inspector. Jobs such as this were cherished jobs and there was much competition for them. As long as you were considered a respectable man, and had a good set of references, you were provided with a house close to the canal.

Jimmy's dad was generally always on hand around Ulverstone, and sometimes he had to work at night, but it was better than the jobs some of his friend's fathers had. Most of *them* worked on the boats, delivering their cargos to far away towns and cities. This meant that they were away from home a lot, and only returning to their families when they had completed a job. Jimmy's dad had once worked on the boats and Jimmy missed him on those cold dark winter nights.

Jimmy waited in the shed while his father unhooked what looked like a pole from a nail on the wall. He came and handed the pole to Jimmy who saw what it was the moment it was dropped into his expectant hands. His dad told him that *he* was given a fishing pole at the same age by Jimmy's grandfather some forty years ago.

The pole was long and smooth. There was a fixed-spool spinning reel attached to it that held fishing twine. His dad then gave him a wicker basket that contained an array of fishing floats, hooks, and weights. Jimmy was so happy with the pole; he'd repeatedly asked his parents for one during the days leading up to Christmas, sadly it didn't materialise. Now here he was in early summer now holding his very own fishing pole. His dad had made the pole for him and had even carved Jimmy's initials into the butt handle.

Because it was early summer, the days were even longer than they were only a week or so ago. Jimmy took his basket and fishing pole and ran all the way over the bank past his house and all the way down to the canal at Wormbridge. He figured that he could spend at least an hour or so fishing before being called in for bed.

He set himself down at the side of the canal: it was peaceful. The boats had long since passed but they had left their greasy film on the water's surface as a reminder to those like Jimmy that the canals and waterways of Ulverstone had a function and a use other than a place to go fishing.

He found a shiny new trowel inside his basket. His dad had put it there and he knew exactly what he was meant to do with it. He began digging on the bank until he found a worm. He eased the worm out of the ground with his fingers and pressed it onto the hook on the end of his fishing twine. He watched the worm as it writhed and wriggled, trying to push itself off the hook, and he wondered briefly, if it was feeling pain before he cast it into the centre of the canal.

Jimmy sat and watched his wine-cork bobber as it sat still on the water. Occasionally, he would reel it in to see if the worm was still attached, happy that the bait was still present he would then cast out his line and the waiting game would start again. He had no idea what he was doing, but he had read enough boys stories and seen enough pictures in the books at the school house to have a basic idea how he was supposed to catch fish. He hoped to be able to bring a large fat fish back to his ma who could cook if for tomorrow's supper.

The sky had been threatening a downpour all afternoon. The clouds had gathered and rolled across the sky as though a giant ink dropper had released its load, spreading until the last shafts of sunlight were sealed. The first giant spots of rain fell and in no time at all the stony path on which Jimmy sat turned into a small stream.

He picked up his fish pole and basket and ran towards the cover of Wormbridge tunnel.

He stood solemnly near the entrance of the tunnel waiting for the rain to subside: It didn't. Even though the tunnel was dark, there was enough light near the opening for Jimmy to see the water clearly, so he decided to carry on with his fishing undercover.

He sat and watched his cork bobber as it was pushed and prodded by the undulating water. The rain was torrential, falling in pick-handles, disturbing the surface as great ripples swelled out and cascaded from one side of the bank to the other. Jimmy saw something floating in the water, the currents had dragged it along through the tunnel. It was a dead duck; blanched bones now showing through rotting plumage.

The duck threatened to disturb Jimmy's float, so he stood to reel it in. It was then that he felt the first tug. He watched as his fishing twine was eaten up by the water at tremendous speed. His fixed-spool reel spun until smoke erupted from it as the twine was dragged further and further below the water. Suddenly the twine reached the end and Jimmy's pole was yanked from his hands. He saw it disappear beneath the pock-marked rainy surface.

Now Jimmy was only ten years old, but he knew that a fishing pole should float. The only pole that could disappear like his just did would have to made of lead. He stood, hands on hips and bent, peering at the water for any trace of his pole. *'Oh my gullygoshers'*, he said aloud as he tried to conceive what kind of a fish could have yanked his pole away. The biggest fish ever caught he imagined, even bigger than the stuffed pike that hung in his cousin's house near Bridgewater. That pike weighed in at Forty-five pounds. It was his cousin's father's pride and joy and that man made sure everyone who entered his house saw it by having it stuffed and hanging it over the hearth.

Jimmy was devastated that he had lost his fishing pole so soon after it had been given to him. What would he tell his father? His father would never believe his story of a monster pike in the canal, big enough to rip a pole from a pair of hands and to drag it down so deep, that no trace of it would ever be seen again. His father would never believe that. His father would be sure to say to him that his story was a *'Skew-wifter if ever I'd heard one,'* and that would be that. No fishing pole. He knew his father would never give him another one, not after he had so carelessly lost the first. The waiting would have to start again, waiting until he was finally old enough to buy his own.

At first, Jimmy thought that a stick or maybe a reed had floated up to the top. The rain had regressed, and the small prong began to rise further from the surface of the water. He stood and watched with incredulity as his fish pole began to rise slowly as though pushed upwards out of the water by an enchantress from an Arthurian legend.

His pole flopped and smacked the water and began to sail away on currents only to be swallowed in the darkness of the tunnel. Then he saw it; the thing that had released his pole. It broke the surface of the water. A thing shaped like a person. An interweaved, matted tangle of slimy pond weed. The thing gave off foul smelling odours of bad gasses and muck. The oily, slippery jumble rose upward and turned to look at him.

It was a thing from out of every childhood terror-story or nightmare, and it was looking right at him. Jimmy let out a startled cry, more of a throaty rattle to be precise as he backed up hitting the cold damp bricks of the tunnel. The bump almost made him topple forwards joining the terror that sat glistening in the slick dark water.

Jimmy ran, and he ran fast, sometimes slipping on the rain-washed grass as he scrambled up the bank. His house was in eyeshot, and he never once looked back: he dare not look back. Jimmy was right about what his father said. His father was angry with him for losing his fish pole, and he gave him extra chores for a week, including cleaning the outhouse.

Jimmy used to walk to school crossing Wormbridge overpass. He would sometimes stop to toss a conker or a stick, or whatever he'd found along the way over the bridge. He loved to hear the satisfying *plop* as it hit the water below. But Jimmy now avoided walking over the bridge, choosing to take the long way around, walking dangerously on the lock beams. He would do anything rather than cross the bit of canal where he had seen the thing that still gave him sleepless nights whenever he saw boatmen cleaning weed from their propellers on a Sunday morning.

***

Wilford was grateful for Jim's story; he wrote it down longhand in his notebook with the intention of typing it out back in his room at the inn. He bought both couples another drink from the bar before leaving the Otter. He cruised *Knotty Buoy* further along the cut to the moorings close to Ulverstone main town.

With his boat secured, Wilford walked into town making his way along the main street flanked either side by an assortment of shops. He bought himself a pair of fleece-lined leather gloves from a gentlemen's outfitters. Next, he entered a shop selling second-hand goods and old curiosities.

Inside the shop he noticed a framed map hanging on the wall near to the counter. He studied the old map and discovered it to be a topographic chart of the entire area of Ulverstone including the waterways. The map looked very old; the lignin in the paper had yellowed with age due to oxidation. He had a more up-to-date map that he had brought with him on this working trip, but it was old maps that would provide him with the information he needed, especially as this one seemed to show all the positions of most of the now, unused canals.

Wilford approached the shopkeeper, a woman in her mid-forties. She had premature grey hair, and a pale complexion to go with it. He asked her if the framed map was for sale. She informed him that it was, and he purchased it for two shillings and sixpence.

With the framed map under his arm, he continued to peruse the articles inside the shop. He examined a wicker basket that was near to the door. The basket was filled with an assortment of old dolls. The sign on the basket read 'Lucky dollies, 2d each.' The shopkeeper watched as he handled one of the dolls She asked if he was a boater. Wilford explained that he had hired a boat for a short spell. He said that he'd noticed that other boats in the area all had similar dolls tethered to their fenders. He asked if she could elucidate why this was the case.

The shopkeeper explained to Wilford that it was a local superstition, that by tying a doll to your boat helped provide safe passage along the waterways and avoid accidents. When He probed further as to the origin of the belief, she simply said, *'That's what folk do around here,'* and finishing with, *'It's all before my time I'm afraid.'* Wilford accepted her deficient explanation and he thought, *when in Rome*, and bought a doll for himself.

Wilford's last port of call was to a fish & chips shop not far from the crossing that led back down to the moorings. The smell of fried fish had made him salivate as he walked along the street. He paid for his fish supper and it was handed to him all wrapped in newspaper by a young man with oily blemished skin. He kept his supper swathed in paper to keep it warm but tore open one end and plucked out the occasional hot fried potato chip as he made his way back to the boat.

Inside *Knotty Buoy*, he first got a fire alight in the stove using the kindling and some coal that Durnsten had left for him. Satisfied that the fire within the green, cast-iron Epping stove was safe to leave without it dying out, he proceeded to finish his fish supper.

As he sat eating out of the newspaper, he noticed a report from the local area informing of a fatal accident near Bridgewater, not far

47

from the Portside Inn. Carefully, he tore the report out from the newspaper sheet, to save it from being ruined by the grease and vinegar that was steadily being soaked up by the printed bundle. As he continued to eat, he read about the accident.

The piece of newspaper that contained the report was from the *Ulverstone Herald*, dated about six months ago. The report read: *'Family mourns loss of father following tragic accident on the water. The wife and son of a Mr. Peter Joseph Adler are devastated following a terrible accident that took Peter's life. According to a work friend, Harry Renshaw, with him at the time on the family boat (a working Dutch barge known locally as Black Bess) Harry said that both he and Peter had been returning from a job in Llangollen when they were busy collapsing a wheel house on the boat to enable them to use a tunnel near Bridgewater. According to Harry Renshaw, 'It was dark, we were getting the wheel house down and had almost finished when this other barge came out of nowhere. It kept on knocking at us like a bull at a gate. Pete went topsaturvey and fell in the water. I looked everywhere, but I could make back-nor-edge of him!' According to Mr. Renshaw, the other barge that caused the collision near the tunnel somehow disappeared, and Mr. Renshaw feared it had capsized.*

The body of Peter Adler was recovered further along the canal near where the old Wormbridge convergence once lay. Jon Welbarrow, a police constable at the scene said of Adler's injuries, 'It looked as though his face had gone through a propeller.' The local coroner said he died due to the fall and appeared to have hit his head, probably on the heavy stonework at Bridgewater tunnel. No wreck of any other boat was discovered at Bridgewater sparking a resurgence of local stories of 'Aggie' the ghostly lady of Wormbridge cut.'

Wilford placed the newspaper report into the back of his notebook. He would include some of the details in his book. He might even attempt to trace the friend of Peter Adler, Harry Renshaw to see if he would be willing to provide a more detailed account of the unfortunate catastrophe.

It was feeling pleasantly warm on the boat with the fire blazing. Outside the temperature had dropped considerably. Wilford glanced through a porthole window set between two wall mounted oil lamps. He shivered as he watched the fog outside as it grew from the water, with its gossamer fingers stroking the hull of the boat, crawling past the window like a threadbare grey shroud. He realised that soon he would be standing there up top, steering *Knotty Buoy* through the thickening miasma.

He contemplated remaining moored where he was and spending the night on the boat, but he was eager to get started on the next section of his book back at the inn. He also hoped to bump into Corinne again.

Corinne had stirred feelings inside him that he had not felt for some time. He wasn't sure he had left the right lasting impression on her and hoped for another chance to make amends. He had spoken about a few controversial things, notably his ramblings about ghosts and writings. Usually he would avoid speaking about these things the first-time meeting somebody he liked. He usually played safe trying to ensure that he came across, '*normal*', and likeable. But he felt safe in her company, she had put him at ease, and he had felt bold enough to let a few things out of the bag. He hoped, that he had remained memorable to Corinne, but not in a bad way.

It was about an hour's cruising back to the inn. It was only six o'clock and Wilford decided that his journey back would take him along the canal where the accident had taken place as mentioned in the newspaper report. He picked up the framed map he had bought earlier. He bent back the staples at the back and removed the backing card. Carefully he removed the map from the frame and set it down on top of the small table where the remains of his supper lay.

He studied the map and got his bearings. He could see the course where he was presently moored quite clearly. The Otter public house was also marked as was the Portside Inn. The map showed a large number of dwellings situated next to the inn, now sadly lost to the passage of time.

On the map, he followed the course of the canal from the Otter towards the Portside Inn. Along the course about halfway, there appeared to be a winding hole, a widened area of the canal used for turning a narrowboat. There was also a junction merging with the main stretch, and there appeared to be a crossing over where the thinner stretch of water joined; the map had this marked as Wormbridge.

Wilford's newer map that he had studied briefly before travelling to Ulverstone didn't show Wormbridge, he'd learned that Wormbridge cut had been drained and filled in. The original bridge-tunnel no longer existed. Happy that he had found Wormbridge on the old map he could at least cruise near to the area where the folk tales originated.

Back on the bank, Wilford began untying his mooring ropes. He noticed how visibility was severely restricted in the dense coverlet of fog. Again, he even thought about staying put, where he was moored, but he much rather preferred the comfort of the inn, than the somewhat hard beds provided on the boat. Throwing the stern rope on the deck, he climbed onboard and turned on both the front and back fog lamps. Both lamps instantly produced a halo of swirling vapour, in no way did they aid visibility. The bright lamps hindered rather than helped, but he knew he had to have them both lit for safety reasons. The last thing he wanted was a collision on the water with another boat.

Using the deck pole, he pushed himself away from the bank, and when safely at sufficient depth he started the engine. The first half mile or so was the toughest. It took a while before his eyes became accustomed to the dark and the fog. Soon he was able to make out the murky shapes of leafless trees on the bank. Lit windows on some of the isolated dwellings resembled blurred orbs of light suspended in the air.

Smoke billowed from *Knotty Buoy's* single smoke stack. The smell from the burning coal below deck was a comfort, filling his nostrils as *Knotty Buoy* chugged leisurely along the cut. He enjoyed the industrial smell that the coal produced when burned. It reminded him of steam trains, and of coal fires lit in houses on damp rainy days. He was thankful he'd been able to buy himself a pair of gloves. He would never have been able to use the tiller to manoeuvre properly without them as the air was freezing.

There had been a couple of times when *Knotty Buoy* had drifted dangerously near the canal banks, the visibility was not improving much as he sailed along. At one point, the loud *'honking'* from a Canadian goose gave him a fright; he'd sailed too close to where it was sleeping on the water and had startled it.

Wilford became aware that the width of the canal had expanded. The murky forms of objects on the banks were further away. He put the engine into reverse and moved the throttle back to reduce the speed of the boat. He was sure he had come to the winding hole at the point of the old junction with Wormbridge.

He stood and attempted to soak up any feelings or ambiances. Things that he might remember when the time came to write about his experiences near to where Wormbridge cut used to branch off from the stretch of water on which he slowly glided. He focused on the sounds, or lack of them other than the noise from the boat itself. He could hear the distinct screech from an owl, and the occasional bark from a distant hound. Sometimes he would hear a *plop* in the water, thinking it to be a large fish briefly surfacing before sinking once more to the cold chilly depths.

Wilford was sure that he could discern a flickering light towards the right side of the bank. He peered through the murk to see what it might be, but the fog lights on the boat polluted his view. He would have ignored the light, passing it off as an illusion created by the fog, and probably nothing more than something reflective caught in the clogged beam of his fog lamp. But then he saw it again, and this time it was duplicated.

Switching off his front fog lamp, he managed to steer the boat towards the flickering lights. He was mindful to keep the speed of the boat to an absolute minimum just in case the lights originated from another boat, and he didn't want any accidents.

With great care he drifted towards the pale, glimmering lights. Now only a few yards away, he was astonished to discover that his boat was facing the mouth of a tunnel. The old brickwork of the tunnel gradually appeared to him from behind the fog's deceptive cape. Each crumbling dark brick revealing itself, each bare twine of ivy and creeper growing more defined the closer he came.

He saw the dancing lights for what they were. Along the towpath, on either side of the tunnel, were lanterns. Each lantern lit by a solitary candle. Each lantern an almost exact replica of the one before it. Wilford rubbed at his eyes; he didn't understand what he was perceiving. It was almost as though the same

54

lantern, copied precisely, was laid out and projected down and deep into the tunnel. He saw that each candle flame flickered in unison with the others as they all burned in impossibly precise timing with one another.

The lanterns were lining the way through the tunnel, almost enticing him to enter and to follow their shimmering path. He now feared that he had become lost on the cut. He had not seen any tunnel on his outward journey. The only tunnel that should rightfully be here was Wormbridge underpass, but as this shaft no longer existed, he realised he must have somehow taken an incorrect diversion.

He put *Knotty Buoy* in reverse, backing away from the tunnel, then he straightened up the best he could under the present unclear conditions. He was now anxious to find out where he was. It would be too difficult to find suitable moorings in these conditions, so whilst the boat was in the middle of the canal and only drifting slowly, he popped below decks to re-stoke the stove. The last thing he wanted was for the fire to go out. He didn't relish being stuck on the boat all night without any warmth *if* being stranded was to be his fate tonight.

With his collar turned up and his fog lamps burning, Wilford continued along the cut in the same direction. He was sure that he hadn't diverted, but he had no explanation for that tunnel, or even, why it was lit so. He was sure that if he kept up good speed then eventually, he would be back at the Portside Inn.

A while later his certitude paid off as he recognised the eves of the inn. There was a lamppost close to the inn that flooded one side with its yellow/orange glow, now in the fog the lamplight was reduced to a mere blush. He guided the boat to the moorings. There were many boats moored up and Wilford had to spend quite a while manoeuvring into his spot. Happy that *Knotty Buoy* was secured for the night, he shut down the stove and collected up his maps before making his way into the inn.

When he got to the door to his room, he had to rummage through all his pockets until he found the key. The door opposite opened and out stepped a middle aged, slightly portly man wearing a tweed suit over a blue striped shirt and navy striped tie. His head was balding but was still sufficiently covered by a bright red neatly parted thatch supported by equally bright bushy eyebrows and an underlining moustache. He nodded towards Wilford, "Good evening, I don't suppose you know if it's too late for supper?" Wilford, still holding his maps cocked his arm higher to read his watch, it read seven forty-five. He hadn't realised how late it was.

"I think you might just be in luck, I believe they stop serving around seven thirty," replied Wilford as he inserted his room-key in the lock.

"Thank you. I will dash down, you see I've been out most of the day and lost track of time." He looked Wilford over and saw how his hair was dripping wet and his coat looked similarly saturated. "Ah, as you must have been yourself!" He added whilst offering his hand, "Preston Haistwell, I'm a guest here, just got here this morning." Wilford took up Preston's hand,

"Wilford, Bailey," he said shaking his hand briefly, "yes, I'm afraid I got caught up in the fog, and I wasn't really dressed for it," explained Wilford.

"Oh yes, the fog this time of year can be quite heavy," Preston saw how Wilford had his hand on his door, eager to get inside and remove his sodden clothing no doubt. "Right, well I think I'll pop down and see what sustenance is on offer, have a good evening," said Preston before locking his room and walking along the landing to the stairs. Wilford slipped inside his room and closed the door. He wasn't that hungry, the fish supper he had earlier sufficed, but he was chilled to the bone and he removed his wet clothing placing it on clothes hangers and hooking them to the picture rail that ran around the room.

Realising it was probably too late to find Corinne in the dining room Wilford ran himself a hot bath. As he soaked, he studied his map guide, the map he brought with him. He folded the map to show a section detailing the stretch of canal he had cruised along. He ran his finger up and along the main cut that flowed around Ulverstone. He found the Otter, but he could find no junctions on the route back that he could have taken by mistake. He could easily find the winding hole that once connected the Wormbridge junction, but the map clearly showed no crossing, tunnel or anything. To put his mind at rest, he decided he would cruise along the canal during daylight hours to see how accurate the map actually was.

***

Wilford entered the dining room of the inn just after eight in the morning. He was tired. He had spent a good portion of the night typing away on his Red Princess. He had embellished the newspaper article to some degree but kept it mostly faithful to the genuine report. He had also written about his own experience along the cut in the fog using suitably imaginative adjectives and similes painting a bleak and somewhat eerie picture for the enticement of his future readers.

He approached the bar and waited for Burt, the Innkeeper, to come over and take his order. Burt put down the wine glass that he was drying with a bar towel and came over to where Wilford stood. "Good morning sir, are you looking for breakfast?" Burt asked.

"Indeed I am. Could I have some bacon and eggs, and perhaps a sausage?" Burt wrote Wilford's order on a small note pad using a pencil.

"Of course sir. Would you like some toast with that?"

"Actually, yes. A round or two if you please," Burt added the toast to the notebook, he then tore off the page.

"Will you be eating at the bar sir?" Wilford glanced around the room, all the tables in the room were clean and laid out with napkins and cutlery. Then he saw Corinne. She was sitting with her back to the room, looking out of a window.

"No, I think I'll sit over there, by the window if I may." He pointed over to where Corinne sat, Burt nodded and told him that he would bring his breakfast over. Wilford thanked Burt then made his way to where Corinne sat.

Wilford stopped behind Corinne, she hadn't seen him approach her, in fact she was unaware he was there at all. Wilford coughed politely, Corinne turned then smiled when she saw him loitering, "May I?" he asked pointing towards the empty chair at Corinne's table.

"Please do Wilford," she said serenely. Delighted that she had remembered his name, he pulled out the chair and sat down.

"I thought I might have seen you here for dinner last night, but I got back quite late," he said.

"Oh? Where had you been?"

"You remember when I told you I'd hired a boat?' Corinne nodded, 'well I had gone to pick it up. It's a real beauty, warm and snug."

"That's nice, I'm glad it went well. I imagine you took the boat out for a spell on the water?"

"Indeed yes, I took him all the way to Ulverstone town. I did a little shopping, but I got caught up that wretched fog. Got a bit lost I think on my way back, but at least I managed to get back," he said. He noticed how Corinne began to frown, and he thought that even with furrows in her brow, she still looked so beautiful.

"Oh dear, that must have been terrifying. I know how thick the fog can be this time of year. Were you alright?"

"Yes, I was just worried I may have a collision or something. The owner of the hire-boat even asked me for quite a deposit, I didn't want to be so stupid as to sink the old boy on my first day."

"Goodness! do boats sink quite often then?" asked Corinne. Wilford smiled then replied jokingly,

"No, usually only once." Corinne chuckled at his attempt at light humour. Burt approached the table carrying Wilford's breakfast. As he set the breakfast down, Wilford noticed the empty plates in front of Corinne. Her cup was also bare.

"Is there anything else I can fetch you sir?" asked Burt.

"Yes, a coffee please, in fact make that two," said Wilford.

"Two sir?" asked Burt. Wilford tilted his head towards Corinne,

"Yes, two if you wouldn't mind." Burt pulled out his notebook and wrote down Wilford's drink order before leaving for the kitchens. Wilford waited for Burt to be out of earshot before he spoke again. "I hope you didn't mind me ordering you a drink, you didn't have one," he said as he began to eat his breakfast.

"Not at all. In fact, it was quite considerate of you." Corinne straightened herself on her seat, "How is your book coming along, the book about the Wormbridge ghost?" Wilford was happy to find that she'd remembered the things they had talked about during their first meeting, and she seemed genuinely happy to talk about them. He could find no reason not to discuss his book.

"It's coming along nicely, thanks for asking. I have a few leads, some people I hope to track down who may be able to offer some first-hand accounts. Although, I have mostly been writing my own thoughts and feelings about the area, the stretch near where the old Wormbridge junction used to be."

"I take it by your words, that there's no longer a Wormbridge junction. Is that so?" Wilford contemplated telling Corinne about his experience last night, how he had found an unmarked tunnel. He decided to mention it, but he would omit the details regarding how the tunnel appeared to be so eerily lit."

"Well, the canal that once ran to Bridgewater, at one time connected to the main Ulverstone stretch, or cut as the Boaters like to say. Thing is, it was apparently drained and filled in about twenty years ago. Even the bridge, the Wormbridge crossing was pulled down I believe." As Wilford finished speaking, Burt returned with a tray containing two cups of coffee and a jug of cream. As he placed the tray down on the table he spoke to Wilford,

"Way I remember, the old bridge just gave way. There was a cart from the local brewery crossing at the time. That cart was heavy, laden with beer kegs. As the bridge crumbled, kegs, horses and driver all went in the drink. Horrible mess it was." Wilford quickly removed his folded map out from his jacket, he politely asked to borrow Burt's pencil so that he could jot down what Burt had said. "They managed to get most of the kegs out,' continued Burt, 'but the driver broke his back, and both horses had to be shot sir." Burt finished his story as he loaded up the tray with the empty plate and other cutlery in front of Corinne.

"I wonder if you could help me?" asked Wilford. "I took my boat out yesterday, all the way into town. On my return journey, I got caught up in the fog somewhat and I think I took a wrong turn somewhere because I came across a tunnel that isn't marked on my map." Wilford set the map down and opened it out, he pushed his breakfast plate away to make more room.

"A tunnel sir?" queried Burt lugubriously.

"Yes, a tunnel, but I simply can't find it on my map." Wilford gestured for Burt to take a closer look as he used his index finger to journey along the narrow lines on the chart. "I came across this winding hole here, and as far as I remember, the tunnel would be on the right as I was facing the way back to this inn." Burt leaned in to take a quick look,

"Well if that's the place you said you were, there's no tunnel sir. The only tunnel that's ever been close was the old Wormbridge pass to Bridgewater. And we both know that old burrow's no longer standing, don't we sir?"

"Are you sure there's no other junction?"

"As sure as I'm standing here sir. Born and bred in these parts as was my father before me, and his father before him sir." Wilford folded his map and put it back in his pocket,

"I just don't understand it. Perhaps it was the fog playing tricks on me," chuckled Wilford.

"Well sir, if I were you, I'd stay moored on foggy nights. These old waterways have a knack for playing games with people foolhardy enough not to treat them with the respect they demand sir. Now, is there anything else I can get for you before I leave?" Wilford shook his head,

"Oh, I just wondered if your good lady wife was feeling any better," he asked.

"She's feeling much better sir, thank you for asking after her."

"Not at all, please give her my best regards."

"I will sir,' said Burt with a smile, 'good day sir." Wilford pulled his breakfast back in front of him and continued to eat.

"I say, I thought old Burt was a little short with you then, don't you think?" spoke Corinne.

"Well, I think you were right Corinne, what you said the other night," spoke Wilford between bouts of eating.

"Oh? What did I say?"

"You said that the locals don't like outsiders poking their nose into their business," answered Wilford as he devoured a sausage.

"I wasn't being serious you know."

"I know, but maybe that's just the case with places like this. Anyway, I'm going to jolly well find out if I was right."

"Whatever do you mean?"

"I'm going to take the long way around to Bridgewater because I want to interview a man who works at a boat repair yard. Last night I read a report in the Ulverstone Herald about an accident he was involved with. I telephoned the local police station before breakfast and managed to get hold of the constable who dealt with the accident. He was able to tell me where the man worked." Corinne looked puzzled,

"I don't understand Wilford, what's an accident got to do with your mysterious tunnel?"

"Nothing really, but he might be able to tell me more facts about the accident which I believe may be loosely connected to the ghost stories and legends around these parts. But I will have a good search for my elusive tunnel whilst I'm out on the cut." Wilford finished his breakfast and drank his coffee whilst Corinne waited. Burt cleared away his plate and cup. "You know, if you haven't anything to do, you could always come with me. Old *Knotty Buoy's* a real delight," spoke Wilford hopefully. Corinne shook her head,

"I'm sorry Wilford, I made a promise to my mother that I would do some jobs for her; she's not as able as she once was. Perhaps another time?" Wilford nodded,

"Of course, you must have plans. It would be nice to meet up for dinner this evening if you'd like to that is?"

"I'm afraid tonight wouldn't be possible, but another night would be lovely," added Corinne.

"Then we shall have dinner another night. How about Thursday?"

"Thursday sounds fine. Are we eating here?"

"Well, we could meet here, say six o'clock, and then decide. How does that sound?"

"It sounds nice Wilford." Corinne and Wilford got up from their table, Wilford pushed in his chair,

"Are you sure I can't persuade you to come with me today?"

"I'm sorry Wilford, it's my mother, I must-"

"You don't have to explain, it's quite alright. It's just so damn lonely on the water, and the weather is so dismal. Thursday night it is, I shall look forward to it." Wilford helped Corinne on with her coat and said goodbye as she left. She waved to him from outside the window and he reciprocated. He noticed she hadn't drunk her coffee and realised that there was so much he didn't know about her, for a start, she was probably a tea drinker. He smiled at the prospect of learning more about Corinne, this little working holiday was turning out to be just the ticket.

Three

The course to Bridgewater was a windy one. At times the wind pushed against the bow and Wilford had to counter the sideways movement by heading *Knotty Buoy* into the wind.

At a point where the canal tapered a little, another narrowboat appeared on the cut up ahead. Wilford had to try exceptionally hard to keep his boat from pivoting and knocking into the passing vessel. It was an equally demanding task for the helmsman of the other boat.

With safe passage for both boats now assured, Wilford raised his hat to the skipper of *Lucky Lady* who responded likewise. For a time, he was followed by a pair of gliding swans. Both birds seemed to keep a beady eye on him, perhaps because they had a nest nearby, or maybe in the hope that he might toss them some bread. Eventually he outran them as a winding hole began to expose itself up ahead.

Wilford reduced *Knotty Buoy's* speed and scanned both banks for any sign of a junction. He thought that this had to be the place where he'd seen the tunnel, lined with lanterns the previous night, yet he was unable to find it.

He looked again and again but Burt was right, there was no convergence with any other channel. As he stood, poised with one hand on the tiller, his cap was whisked off his head by the wind only to land on the water some distance to his left. He watched in exasperation as it drifted away and he began following it, battling the wind's determination to keep him from reclaiming it.

He pushed *Knotty Buoy* dangerously close to the bank on the left of the winding hole. The wind was threatening to hem him up in a prickly bush. He used the deck pole to shove himself away from the bank and the tangle of thorns that was becoming ever so more imperilling.

His hat had got lost in a mesh of weeds and reeds near to the bank and he had lost sight of it. He decided to accept his loss and was about to give himself one final push away from the bank with the deck pole when he noticed something. On the grassy bank, amongst a clump of fading nettles, was a small pile of five or more red bricks.

He saw some more bricks scattered about on the surface of the bank, many were overgrown by ivy, moss, and long grass but the further he looked the more he could see. He wondered if these bricks were the last reminders of the old tunnel at Wormbridge.

As he surveyed the grassy bank, he noted how it rose higher than the bank on the opposite side of the winding hole. If this was the site of the old Wormbridge linkup, then he was looking at the earth that had been shoehorned in to seal it up, preventing the force of water within the vast expanse of the winding hole from breaking down the bank and reclaiming the disused route.

As he stood and examined the neglected and abandoned scene before him, he knew that he couldn't possibly be at the same place as he was the previous night. He must have gone off route in the fog, but his map gave no other options. This conundrum perturbed him as he sailed further out into depth within the winding hole.

***

The Bell boatyard was revealed to Wilford as he proceeded along the cut towards the locks. The Lock he had to pass through was a course that led downhill. He left *Knotty Buoy* in neutral placed at the front of the lock. He checked that the front fender was secured properly before jumping onto the path and walking to the end of the lock gate.

A lockkeeper on site came to aid Wilford as he attempted to operate the lock singlehanded. The lock was devoid of water beyond the gates, and together they checked all the lower paddles were closed before winding up the top ones. Gradually, the water was let in.

Once the water level had risen, they pushed open the gates and wound the paddles down again. Wilford jumped back onboard *Knotty Buoy* and sailed into the now filled lock, the keeper then closed the gates behind him. Wilford thanked the keeper before moving on towards the Bell boatyard.

Wilford moored his boat off a small jetty constructed from timber staging. He made his way along the staging towards a large workshop cladded with green somewhat rusting corrugated iron sheets. The workshop had bright red life rings hanging from hooks in a line around the structure. Surrounding the workshop were a series of paved and shingle paths running beyond the quay heading.

The water was filled with an assortment of vessels, all lined up like dead men in the water. Some larger boats were tethered to trots that were permanently fixed to the river bed.

On the front of the workshop was a large sign with the word *'OFFICE'* inscribed. Below this sign was a smaller notice proclaiming the office to be *'OPEN'*.

Inside the workshop, he made his way over to a workbench where a short stocky man with a wild white beard was busy making repairs to a rudder. Wilford asked the man where he could find Harry Renshaw. The man stopped work on his rudder for a moment so that he could point to a door at the back of the workshop, "You'll find 'Arry back there, he's blackin' round back," said the man before resuming his work.

Wilford stepped through the door at the back and saw a yard filled with boats of diverse descriptions all on dry platforms in various stages of restoration and repair. He spotted a man who was applying a coat of bituminous black paint to the underside of one narrowboat. Assuming this was Harry Renshaw, he walked over to greet him.

Wilford held out his hand in a friendly gesture to Harry, "Good morning, would you be Harry Renshaw by any chance?" Harry plopped his paintbrush down into the bucket of black bitumen. He glanced Wilford over several times, but he didn't take Wilford's hand.

"I won't shake hands wi' yer, not unless you want 'ands as black as mine," he said turning his hands over so that Wilford could see how black they were.

"Yes, oh I see. Are you Harry Renshaw?" asked Wilford again.

"I might be, who's asking?" said Harry defensively.

"My name's Wilford Bailey. I understand you were involved in an accident a few months ago, an accident that saw the sad death of your colleague, Peter Adler." Wilford watched as Harry reached into his pocket to withdraw a pewter hip flask. He unscrewed the cap and took a swig. Wilford noticed that Harry's nose was swollen, red, and bumpy, he guessed it was probably due to Rhinophyma, or as some called it, *'drinker's nose'*. Wilford surmised that Harry probably liked the grog a little too much.

"You a copper?" harry asked and took another mouthful from his flask.

"No, no I'm not the police. I'm looking into the unfortunate mishap that you both suffered."

"Well if you're not police, why're you lookin into what happened?"

"I came here from Oxford, you could say that I am a chronicler of mythos. It's how I make my living." Wilford could see that Harry didn't understand what he had just told him, his blurred, bloodshot eyes gave a blank expression. Wilford took out his wallet and pulled out a five-pound note. He held it up for Harry to see.

"I'll pay you for your time. All I want is a little information. Your story of the accident, nothing more. Then I'll be on my way and you'll be five pounds better off," said Wilford. Harry eyed the paper note,

"You're willing to pay five pounds for a story eh?"

"Yes, that's all I want, your account of what happened."

"My story's important, is it?"

"I think so Mr Renshaw, I really do."

"If it's that important, reckon you might pay ten pounds," added Harry cheekily. Wilford frowned,

"I think five pounds is a very good offer. I see you like your drink,' said Wilford as Harry took another suck from his flask. "You could buy more with five pounds," Wilford enticed.

"Aye, and even more with Ten." Realising that he would get nowhere without giving in to Harry, Wilford pulled out another five-pound note and handed them both to Harry. Harry's eyes lit up, and for a moment, Wilford could see the man he used to be, before the rum had ravaged his body and soul so many years ago.

"Now I've given you what you want, will you tell me what I want to know?" Wilford pulled out his notebook and pencil and waited for

Harry to finish drinking from his flask once again.

Harry led Wilford over to a couple of upturned crates, they both sat on them using them as stout, but rickety seats. Harry began to relate how he and Peter had been returning from a job in North Wales when they had almost reached home at the other end of Bridgewater. He described how they had both folded down the wheel house on the barge, so they could pass through the tunnel, and how another boat somehow had appeared behind them without either of them noticing. "I mean, we ought to have heard it," said Harry, "but neither of us did. One minute we were both alone on the cut, next minute we were rammed like!"

"This other boat rammed into yours?" asked Wilford.

"Aye, not too hard, but hard enough to knock old Pete into the bath. Head first he went in. It was then I saw the other boat, well, when I say saw the other boat, what I mean is, the other boat had gone, vanished as though it had niver been close."

"The other boat just disappeared, right in front of you?" Wilford attempted to get all of Harry's story into his notebook, and at times to the detriment of neatness.

"Aye, just like a magician's trick it was. But I wasn't really watching, I was trying to get old Pete out the bath." Harry drained more rum from his flask before continuing, "I niver told the copper everything. I thought he might think I was drunk on the job or a madman. I thought he might think I did for old Pete. I was scared they might say I killed him!" Harry began to look worried, "Look, you said you weren't a copper, right?"

"I wasn't lying Harry, I'm not the police. I'm not here to accuse you of anything, I just want you to tell me what happened. Everything you can remember." Harry sucked the last of the rum from his flask and replaced the empty ampule back into his pocket.

"I'll niver forget it, niver! I searched for Pete and saw him face down in the bath, laid out like a lettuce he was. His head was slanting down, completely in the water. It looked like he was being drawn away by something, something under the water. I reached for the boathook, I was able to hook it onto Pete's foot, his boot. I couldn't hold onto him though. Whatever had hold of Pete, it was strong." Harry began to appear nervous; his hands began to tremble. "I lost the hook to the water, pulled clean out me hands. Last thing I remember of Pete was the soles of his boots as they were swallowed up in the tunnel." Harry's eyes began to brim with tears, but these tears weren't due to the loss of his friend Peter Adler, they were tears born out of absolute terror.

Wilford noted Harry's quivering hands as he continued to recount his experience. "I know many folks would think me daft, but I reckon that it be the work of Aggie. Aye, it was old Aggie who got Pete."

"You mean the ghost lady of Ulverstone?" asked Wilford.

"Aye, that's what I mean. Since that night I keep off the water, I work for my brother Malcolm now. I survived see, but I feel ... stained. Not many people live to tell a tale of old Aggie. I know of only one other, just the two of us there are." Wilford stopped writing, he could see that Harry was growing more anxious by the minute.

"What do you mean you feel stained?" he asked Harry.

"I mean, Aggie knows I was with Pete. I bet she wanted us both, but I wasn't taken, not that night. Folks around here have a saying, they say that Aggie will 'cut your lights out and leave your liver int' dark', they say that about anyone who says they saw her and lived to tell it."

"You said you know of another. Do you mean another person who has seen Aggie and lived to tell?"

"Aye, old Elsie, she's as mad as an odd duck. Lives up at Keeper's Cottage on Damdike Bank. She's old, if she's a day over ninety." Wilford spent a while recording everything that he could remember that Harry spoke of. Whilst he scribbled his notes in his book, Harry began looking about the boatyard, wringing his hands as though something was troubling him.

"She don't like it when she's talked about, folks say," added Harry quietly.

"Who? You mean Elsie?"

"No. I mean Aggie." Harry stood from his crate, he carried on searching for something as though expecting to find it. "Once I was working with Arthur on a boat back here, cleaning the hull of muck and grime before blacking. I was talking about Aggie, what I saw. It wasn't long after Pete's death. The boat me and Arthur worked on just toppled over, crushed Arthur near to death it did. Said it was just an accident they did. Said it was a rotten prop pole they did."

A man wearing a dark grey donkey jacket left the workshop and with a purposeful stride, he came over to where Wilford and Harry now stood. Harry began scratching his head nervously,

"Stop scratching your head, you'll get splinters in your fingers." Said the man wearing the donkey jacket. He asked Harry why he had stopped working. Harry introduced the man to Wilford as his brother. He told Malcolm that Wilford had come to interview him and to pay him for his time.

"What, interview our Harry? What about?" Malcolm asked.

"About the accident, the accident with Pete," added Harry.

"You police?" asked Malcolm. Wilford shook his head and was about to speak but Harry spoke for him,

"He's a chronic of midas, or summit like," explained Harry erroneously.

"Chronic my arse! A reporter more like." Wilford disputed that he wasn't a reporter. "Look, do you have a boat needs fixing? If not, then I reckon you should be on your way," spat Malcolm. He then told Harry to return to his work. Harry trundled away leaving Wilford standing, feeling awkward. "Well, have you a boat needs fixing?" Wilford told Malcolm that he would be on his way. He thanked Harry for the information he had given him before leaving the yard under the watchful eyes of Malcolm.

Wilford sailed *Knotty Buoy* back through the lock and moored up not too far away from where the Bell boatyard sat. He used a stake for temporary mooring, driving the stake into the bank using a club hammer. He slanted the stake away from the boat to ensure that the boat didn't pull the pin out and start drifting.

There was a handy convenience store nearby up the bank and he collected a few items: some bread, cheese, tea, biscuits, and milk. He would have his lunch on the canal today.

He had brought his typewriter on board as he intended to spend some time working on his book. His typewriter was a noisy contraption, and now he had a neighbour, (Preston Haistwell) occupying the room opposite his own, he thought he might end up with some protests if he carried on working through the night as he had been doing.

Wilford had spent a couple of hours typing out as much as he could remember about what Harry had told him, he also began work with generating descriptions of the canal courses around Ulverstone. He decided to take a break, as he was beginning to experience some of the regular wrist pain that he had started to suffer with in recent months. He blamed his aches and pains on the amount of typing he regularly did, and he had occasionally taken up the practice of wearing a wrist strap which seemed to alleviate his discomforts.

He had continued to keep the Epping stove well stoked as he worked; the coal was glowing red hot inside the mini furnace. He filled a copper kettle from his water tank and set it on the stove.

Looking out of the porthole near to where he had been sat working, he could see that the wind was still strong. The trees on the bank were bending in the gusts that were bellowed towards them with regularity. The boat rocked with each new blast and he checked frequently to see if the mooring stake was still holding firm.

He made himself a pot of tea and brought the pot; cup and tea strainer, and bottle of milk over to his work table. Then he carved himself some bread and cheese. He sat and ate whilst reading over what he had written, making some corrections with a pencil where necessary.

A squally shower or two swept over the boat whilst he ate his lunch. The sky was turning darker, and it was only two-thirty if the clock mounted between two brightly burning oil lamps was to be believed.

The cosiness brought on by the Epping stove made him feel somewhat sleepy. He closed his eyes after he'd drained the last mouthful of tea from his cup. With his arms folded across his chest he drifted into a deep slumber.

***

Harry Renshaw had finished his work at the Bell boat yard at four-thirty. He was making his way to the White Horse Tavern along the towpath that grew out from the Bell boatyard. He intended to spend some of the money that Wilford had paid him on beer. The rest he would keep and buy himself a bottle of rum from the off-license in town.

His brother Malcolm had reprimanded him over being caught chatting with Wilford during his working hours. Malcolm was his older brother; however, he was also his boss, and the relationship they both had at the Bell was strictly one of employer and underling. Harry didn't get any preferential treatment over his co-workers because of his family ties with Malcolm. Malcolm didn't hold Harry in much regard, he knew he had a drink problem, and he knew that he could be unreliable, and frequently turn up for work late. The quality of his work too was always in question.

Malcolm knew that Harry was a liability and he knew that he should have fired him almost as soon as he had started to work at the boatyard. But Harry had little to offer any employer. Without his job at the Bell he would probably end up impoverished and adrift like the very boats he worked on, floating from one place to another, lying under dark tunnels where the damp droplets of water would wake him in the morning and dampen him during the night.

Malcolm couldn't condemn Harry to an early grave; Harry had troubles. Whether those troubles came solely out of old green bottles, or from elsewhere, the fact was they were troubles, demons that Harry had to deal with.

Harry had told his brother that he couldn't go back to his old job, hauling coal on a barge, not after what had happened to Pete. The thing was, Harry was terrified. As a child, he had soaked up all the stories about *Aggie*, many of them came from Elsie Hardwicke; the wife of the old lockkeeper over at Damdike Bank.

Harry's mother helped Elsie look after the local church. They swapped knitting patterns for shawls and gloves, and the occasional pullover, knitted for Harry. His mother often sent him on errands to Elsie's cottage. When Harry arrived at the cottage, Elsie would always greet him and give him a hard-boiled egg. Elsie kept chickens, and during the war when eggs were hard to come by, Harry enjoyed receiving them for his troubles.

Sometimes Harry would stay and play a while with Elsie's younger daughter Betty; they were the same age, and Betty was more like a boy than a girl, choosing to climb trees or skim stones across the surface of the canal. Sometimes Harry and Betty would sit by the fire on a threadbare Rag-rug that Elsie had made and listen to her warnings and stories about *Aggie*.

Elsie told them that she had been one of the lucky ones, in that she'd survived an encounter with *Aggie* when she was a little girl while on her father's boat. Elsie claimed that the lord god had spared her for a purpose, so that she could warn everyone else.

She told them that mocking *Aggie*, like some of the gypsy boys did was asking for trouble. She told Harry that the gypsy boys would cuss and holler whenever they played near Wormbridge, shouting out all manner of '*dirty language*', as Elsie called it. She said if ever she caught one of them boys, she would rub a soap bar in his mouth until he foamed like a rabid dog. Harry never doubted it.

Elsie always told all the kids to '*Be good, and if you can't be good, be careful*'. But it was always the warning she gave about what *Aggie* would do to a child out late, when he shouldn't be out late; out late and up to mischief. '*She'll cut your lights out and leave your liver int' dark*'. Harry would lie in his bed back at home wondering what that actually meant.

As he walked along the path the wind was beginning to make his temples ache. He rubbed at his head whilst whistling Moonlight Cocktail, by Glenn Miller, a favourite tune of his. As he walked, he began to experience a feeling that he was being watched. He tried to ignore it at first, but that nagging feeling, that sensation of prickling skin, of cold clammy sweat beading on his back.

Harry whistled louder, he sunk his hands deeper into the pockets of his donkey jacket, he hung his head low and even began turning his head ever so slightly away from the bank on the opposite side of the canal. He could see the shape from his peripheral vision. He tried to ignore it as it hung there, suspended over the wind flattened grass that looked all brown in the moonlight.

His foot snagged on something, he couldn't stop himself falling forwards hitting his face on the edge of the path before plunging into the chilly water. Submerged up to his midback, he kicked his leg and struggled to free his foot that had somehow been caught up in a loop on a badly tied mooring rope.

Harry tried to sit up, to pull himself up using his stomach muscles but failed each time only to serve himself another ducking into the gritty water. His head was now permanently immersed under about a foot of water, the air escaping from his lungs rippled the surface of the water, distorting the moon's bright sickle shining over him.

As the life ebbed away from his body, he saw something blot out the moonlight; something close, standing over where his bent body lay dangling. The last thoughts that passed through his failing mind were Elsie's words, *'She'll cut your lights out and leave your liver int' dark'*.

85

***

Wilford woke with a start. The wind had whipped up the water under *Knotty Buoy* and as the boat rocked, he was slammed into the side of the hull. The oil lamps were still burning but the fire in the stove was almost out. He glanced at the clock: it read a quarter to five.

The first thing he did was to check that he was still moored to the bank. Relieved that he was, he set to work reviving the fire, little by little with the odd chunk of coal and opening the vents to get a good draw. Soon the fire had new life and was beginning to heat up the space below decks.

He hadn't intended to sleep for so long and began to wonder if in fact it was due to toxic fumes from the stove itself. Leaving those thoughts till later, he wrapped himself up warm before untethering the boat from the mooring stake and pushing himself out into the mid cut.

Wilford steered the boat the best he could. Unlike the previous night, there was no fog, the strong winds had blown it all away, but the winds themselves posed new complications.

Like the outward journey, the wind made sailing difficult, pushing him sideways, and threatening to pivot the boat. Soon the banks rose a little and the cut was shielded by tall poplar trees offering Wilford a respite from the challenges thrown at him.

Soon he found himself gliding into the winding hole where earlier in the day he had lost his hat. Glancing at the bank on his right he saw a flickering light. This time he allowed the wind to gently nudge him over to the bank where to his astonishment, he again saw the same bridge and tunnel that he had encountered in the fog the previously.

Controlling the boat, he remained in a position that allowed him to study the manifestation. The tunnel, was like a vast mouth inhaling, drawing him closer inside. He knew this tunnel didn't exist on the map, and furthermore, he knew it wasn't there when he had examined this stretch of the bank earlier.

Wilford was beginning to doubt his own rationality. Is it possible that he could be suffering from some medical condition? Some form of insanity? He began to feel afraid, feeling his own mortality begin to degrade and decay like the dilapidated brickwork that continued to beckon him, drawing him in.

The wind caused *Knotty Buoy* to pivot so that now Wilford faced the tunnel. He could see the same line of lanterns burnishing the interior of the tunnel with their uncanny, weak lustre.

He wanted to drive himself into the tunnel, yet he dare not. He dare not because the tunnel was not meant to be here. It was an impossible tunnel yet here it was standing before him. The flickering lanterns all dancing in synchronisation enticed him to enter as though they were telling him not to worry, he was safe, safe as long as he followed the lanterns all the way inside and beyond.

Once he had crossed the brink, there was no turning back. He felt the drops of water hit his scalp with regularity. Water filtered through brickwork, cold, oily water. The water was real, he could feel it. The tunnel was real.

He noticed how ethereal the lanterns looked and he held out a boathook in an attempt at raising one off the glistening tow path; however, the hook passed through the lantern only to reveal its lack of substance. This alone would have been enough to instil fear within his heart, but as he replaced the boathook on the deck, he now saw the glare from a lamp some distance ahead.

At first a mere pinpoint, a speck that grew in brightness and clarity. Wilford realised that it had to be the lamp from a boat on the water; a boat heading towards him.

Suddenly, and without warning, the engine on *Knotty Buoy* died, and both his front and rear headlamps were extinguished. Here he now stood, shrouded in total darkness, without so much as a warning light. Fearing a collision, he dived below decks and searched about wildly for a torch or anything he could use to signal to the oncoming boat.

Wilford could find nothing below decks that could be useful. He climbed back on deck, now the light was even closer. Because it was merely a glare and some way out in front, he had no way of knowing how far away it really was. Picking up the deck pole he tried to use it to push his boat backwards. He began to have some success as *Knotty Buoy* slowly inched back, but the problem was the wind.

The wind was shoving the boat from the stern, forcing it further into the tunnel. He jumped down onto the tow path and grabbed hold of a mooring rope. He tried to pull the boat back using all his strength, but he soon felt exhausted. He wondered that if he had two lungs would it have made a difference? Could a man drag such a weight against the wind?

Whilst he was down on the path, he stopped briefly to examine one of the ghostly lanterns. Each was spaced about five yards apart. He dragged his foot through one of them, its image distorted briefly as though made of smoke, only this smoke would coalesce and reform the boxy shape the moment his foot had passed through it.

Wilford clambered back on the boat. So far, he had failed to manoeuvre it using the ropes, and the pole had little or no effect. The light in the distance burned bigger and brighter; he noticed that it had the same indistinct gleam that was provided by the lanterns on the paths either side.

He had to get a warning out to the approaching boat, to avert a collision. He remembered that there was a horn at the bow. He ran over and pressed the push button starter, but the horn was mute. There was no auxiliary power to sound it. In frustration, he hit the starter over and over.

Cupping his hands around his mouth Wilford called out, "Hey! hey stop the boat!" over and over. As the light came even nearer, Wilford braced himself for the inevitable bump.

If it wasn't for the rope fenders, Wilford's boat probably would have sustained substantial damage. The strike jolted *Knotty Buoy*. Wilford lost his balance and toppled forward face down on the deck. There was a slight cracking splintering sound, but nothing too unsettling. Wilford scrambled to his feet, knowing that the hull of *Knotty Buoy* was primarily constructed from metal, he feared the other boat had come off worse.

Unable to see anything of the boat that was now butted against his; the glare of its bow mounted headlamp was blinding him, Wilford called out. "Hey, are you alright? It's my fault, my engine cut out, I'm sorry." He stopped speaking when the smell became overpowering.

It was an odour of burning, a stench so strong Wilford had to shield his nose and mouth with his hand. He was afraid that the collision had caused a fire, maybe one of the oil lamps below decks on his boat had been knocked down during the impact, or perhaps, the Epping stove.

He dashed down below deck to check. Both lamps were still mounted on the wall, the stove was also undamaged. There was a lot of broken crockery that had fallen from shelves and cupboards, but otherwise, everything looked sound. Realising that the burning must be coming from the other boat he hurried back up top.

Wilford crossed from his bow, to the bow of the other boat. Immediately, once he had passed the glare from the headlamp, he was able to see the devastation of this vessel. The decking, wheelhouse, practically everything, was charred and steaming. Wilford could feel the heat penetrating through the soles of his shoes as he carefully walked over the carbonised blackened deck planks.

He called out again weakly saying he was here to help, but he had to stop constantly to resist a gagging reflex; the stink of the smouldering boat was so intense, like thousands of burning wet cigars, and just when he thought that he could no longer bear it, the screaming began.

It rang out and seemed to penetrate and reverberate deep inside his skull. It was the agonised tortured cries, of a creature, a man, or a thing. It sounded as though whatever was producing the pitiful howls was doing so as though something had been placed into the unfortunate's mouth, to silence or prevent the yells.

Suddenly, a new, inorganic groaning sound issued. This new sound was produced by the charred boat as it began to thrust into *Knotty Buoy*, shoving him backwards along the tunnel. Fearing for his own vessel, Wilford leapt back on his boat and took up a position holding the tiller, steering as best as he could, avoiding colliding with the stone paths either side as his boat was forced backwards at ever increasing speed.

Soon Wilford had been dislodged from the tunnel, his boat pivoted, sending him into a near 180-degree turn as he entered the winding hole. Once he had levelled the boat, he glanced back, he could not see the other boat at all, but what was even more disturbing, was the complete lack of any tunnel. The underpass opening had ceased to be.

Drifting silently within the winding hole, propelled only by the wind's bluster, Wilford stood staring towards where that tunnel should have been. Convinced that he was now suffering from a disorder of his mind, he almost wept. It was the memory of his grandfather that now crawled across the vision centres of his mind, like a sickening spider dragging itself out from its shady hidey-hole. A memory he had hidden, tucked away, out of sight, out of mind.

His paternal grandfather, the senior Wilford Bailey, had succumbed to a severe and fatal form of dementia. Before his death, he had become a shadow of the man he was, and barely a shadow. His last days where he was still able to communicate with his family were spent in a fantasy world of his own construction.

Wilford had tried hard to suppress the memories that terrified him as a small child. To see his grandfather become transformed, becoming a drooling skeletal figure, constantly soiling himself. And those deadpan eyes, staring at the back of a door, not seeing the door, seeing beyond the door, as though watching a scene played out only unto him.

His grandfather was only fifty-four when he began to experience the first symptoms. Sometimes forgetting where he had left an item such as a walking cane, or a hat. Soon the condition had worsened, and he couldn't remember the names of his nearest and dearest. Wilford was only in his thirties, was his grandfather's condition inherited? He simply could not accept that he should be losing his faculties at such a relatively young age.

Wilford tried the engine over and over, and on the eleventh try, much to his delight, it started. He steered the boat back out of the winding hole and along the course that headed back to the inn. He had not travelled more than a few hundred yards when the engine died again.

Frustrated, he thumped the tiller, both his front and rear lamps were out again. Then he saw a glare reflecting from off the metallic bulb holder on the rear lamp. He turned and could see a shimmering light some way off behind on the water; luminosity expanding as it came closer. It was the light cast from the headlamp of a boat.

Terrified that the same marauding vessel he'd encountered in the tunnel was now in pursuit of him, he tried desperately to start *Knotty Buoy's* engine. Alas, *Knotty Buoy* was a stubborn soul and refused to stir. Each time Wilford glanced back, the approaching boat was gaining on him. He felt his heart race, and his solitary lung was working double time to provide him with the much-required extra air that his jittery frame needed.

The other vessel shrouded behind a shield of incandescent glare could now be heard, its tireless engine, a choppy clockwork chug-chug-chug as it came dangerously closer still.

Wilford shouted a warning towards the boat, but like last time, in the tunnel, he feared it would not stop. He pressed the horn starter and was relieved to hear a loud blast issue from it. When he eventually removed his hand, the horn continued to sound, it was then he realised that his horn was still mute. The sound still blasting through the frosty air was coming from the approaching boat. It was then that Knotty Buoy suddenly spluttered into life.

With both rear and front headlamps burning, Wilford watched as the other barge that had the name *Edna's Angel* scripted across its hull, glided past him. An elderly man and a woman who Wilford presumed to be his wife, perhaps with the name Edna, were both shouting profanities at him as they breezed by.

He slowed down his boat to allow the quicker passage of Edna's Angel whose occupants still cussed relentlessly until only the rear lamp with its misty halo could be seen edging further into the distant darkness. Relieved that the other boat was not the same unsettling craft that he had encountered in the impossible tunnel, he pushed *Knotty Buoy* full throttle, intending to make it back to the inn as swiftly as possible.

With the boat moored for the night, Wilford locked the cabin doors. He checked over the boat for any sign of damage. Everything looked to be in good order. The only sign that indicated an encounter with the charred boat in the tunnel was the ragdoll he'd bought at the shop the previous day. The doll was no longer intact. The body of the doll had been sheared in two; stuffing was spilling out from the neck and the midriff; both parts were still secured to the rope fender. He carried the case containing his portable typewriter inside the inn.

It was only early evening when Wilford entered his room. He set the typewriter down on the desk and removed his coat. He rubbed his hands over his face, and when he removed them, he studied them and watched how they trembled ever so slightly. He needed something to calm his nerves, he was still anxious that he might be experiencing signs of early senility.

He noticed that his room had been tidied during the day. The bed was neatly prepared and turned down slightly. He saw that there was a note resting on the pillow.

He quickly unfolded the note to read it. The note informed him that whilst he had been out on the water, he had received a telephone call. A number was written on the note. Wilford recognised the number to be that of his publisher's office. Realising that the office would now be closed, he decided to return the call in the morning after breakfast. Still requiring something to calm his anxiety, he locked his room and went downstairs to the bar.

Four

Wilford had ordered himself a large glass of brandy and proceeded to drink it all down in one gulp. He then ordered another. Burt wasn't behind the bar tonight, instead, a younger man with a receding dark hairline was on duty. He eyed Wilford apprehensively as Wilford continued to guzzle his brandy, but his worry was lifted when he saw a familiar patron approach Wilford with a friendly manner.

"I say it's Mr Bailey isn't it?" said Preston as he greeted Wilford. "Forgive me, but I'm rather useless with names I'm afraid." Wilford stared at the little man, the effects of the drink were beginning to take effect, subduing his alertness slightly. He shook his head and was about to apologise to Preston for not recognising him, but then he remembered.

"Ah, I'm sorry, it must be the brandy. Preston Haistwell, I think you said. My neighbour upstairs, that's right isn't it?"

"Yes, indeed. We spoke briefly yesterday evening," recalled Preston, "you were saturated by the fog." Wilford nodded,

"Yes, that's right. No fog tonight." Wilford noticed that Preston was carrying a case with a strap. "Are you planning on having a drink?" Wilford asked him.

"I was as it happens," replied Preston.

"Then allow me to buy you one," said Wilford, and he caught the attention of the bartender. "What would you like? A Scotch or ..."

"A Scotch would be nice, thanks," said Preston as he sat on a bar stool next to Wilford. The bartender brought them both a drink, Preston used a jug to add water to his Scotch. He watched as Wilford finished his current drink and then gulped down his latest,

"Down the hatch," Wilford said then called the bartender over again. "Another?" Wilford asked Preston. Preston nodded and reluctantly he finished his own drink just in time before the replacement arrived. "Burt not on duty tonight?" Wilford asked the younger barman."

"No, my father-in-law's at home with his wife, she's been unwell," replied the barman.

"Oh, I thought Burt said that she was getting better?"

"She is sir, but he wanted to spend an evening or two at home, make sure she was being looked after."

"Very wise, send them both my regards when you next see Burt will you," said Wilford and this time both men carried their drinks over to a table by a window. Preston set his case down on the table before sitting himself down. Wilford wobbled slightly before dropping himself into a sturdy chair.

Both men chatted for a while about the Portside Inn, about how comfortable their respective rooms were, and about the good food. Wilford asked Preston if this was his first visit to the Inn. "No, no I make frequent visits to Ulverstone. I've been coming here, to the Portside for over eight years." Wilford told Preston that this was his first stay in the area. He then asked Preston why Ulverstone had captivated him enough to have him return so often. Preston opened the small case he had with him and revealed a camera.

"I'm a photographer, started as a hobby but now I guess you could say that I'm semi-professional. I sell a lot of my work to magazines, and the public buy them." Realising that Preston was a lot more interesting than he had first thought after their initial meeting on the landing, Wilford probed further,

"What do you take photographs of? I mean, what is your subject? Wildlife?"

"I do take wildlife picture as it happens. But not only wildlife. I do portraiture and landscapes mostly. I don't know if you noticed the photograph hanging midway up the stairs to the floor above?" Wilford shook his head. "I took that picture of the Portside Inn and I gave it to Burt." Wilford hadn't noticed a photograph, but he made a mental note to do so on his way up to his room later.

Preston turned the camera he was holding over in his hands and spoke of it admiringly. "This is a Mighty Hit sub-miniature, with telephoto lens. I also use a Mercury Two, but this one is my preferred choice. I obtained it during a holiday in America." Wilford leaned in to show a bit of interest, but he didn't know anything about cameras, one looked very much like another to him. "I came here to try and get a picture of something that's been eluding me for many years,"

"Oh, and what's that?" asked Wilford. Preston replaced the camera back into its case.

"There is reported to be something very special along the stretch of canal, just up by Bridgewater. I daresay you wouldn't know about it, but I've been trying to capture one on film for many years, unsuccessfully so far

I'm afraid to say." Wilford's interest picked up, there was only one thing famous enough around Ulverstone that could keep a man obsessed. He thought that Preston must be referring to the ghost of *Aggie.*

"I think I know what you are looking for. You see, I'm also interested in the same thing," said Wilford almost breathless with excitement. Preston's eyes widened with surprise,

"Well bless my soul, are you also trying to get a sighting of the king?"

"King? I don't understand. I thought-"

"Ah, late morning. Now you see to be honest that's the only time I've ever really seen them, between about seven and eleven. Never had my camera ready. Sod's law I think they call it," said Preston. Wilford gave him a blank look as he continued. "I have no idea if there are any youngsters as I haven't seen any, but next time I do I will have my camera ready, there is no doubt. And you Wilford, have you had any luck? Are you in a twitching club?"

"Twitching?" replied Wilford still unenlightened at Preston's inferences.

"Yes, a twitcher, well that's what they call our kind of enthusiast don't they? Or do you prefer the term birdwatcher?" Preston who could read the puzzled face of the man opposite him now began to realise that they had both gotten their wires crossed. "You're not here for the kingfishers?" he said finally. Wilford smiled, suddenly everything was clear,

"Ah, I see. You are looking for kingfishers, no I'm afraid I'm not here for the same thing at all," he said chuckling. Preston looked a little foolish,

"I thought that would be too much of a coincidence, yes, too much. Then what are you here for, if you don't mind me asking?" Wilford explained that his time here was spent doing some research for a book he was writing, and when Preston pushed him to elaborate about his book, Wilford provided him with an explanation of the legend surrounding Ulverstone, and particularly, Wormbridge cut.

Preston showed a great deal of interest in the tales of *Aggie*. When Wilford had finished with his explanation he waited for Preston's response. He gave it with great enthusiasm. "Well, what an interesting preoccupation you certainly have," he said.

"Do you think so?"

"I certainly do. I have always loved a good old ghost yarn, but who doesn't? Of course, I like to read ghost stories myself." Wilford smiled, glad that he hadn't received any ridicule for the disclosure of the subject matter of his books. "I enjoyed reading the Signalman by Dickens, that scared the wits out of me I must say, oh, and then there's the

Turn of the Screw, another terrifying tale don't you think?" Wilford nodded in agreement,

"Yes, I agree, they are both good works, but I don't actually write fiction myself, I merely relate the tales passed on to me, hand to mouth."

"I imagine you have collated some good ones. I have to say that I haven't heard of the stories you mentioned, I've been coming to the area for many years and nobody has spoken about Aggie to me."

"Both you and I are outsiders. In places like Ulverstone, people tend to be a little reticent," explained Wilford.

"So, tell me, have you managed to obtain any evidence of Aggie, any proof as it were to corroborate the stories?" Wilford wasn't sure how to answer Preston. He wondered if he should tell him about his puzzling and fear-provoking experiences with the tunnel, or even with the charred boat.

"No evidence, at least … nothing concrete, up to now." Wilford finished his drink and his attention began to wander. Preston was no trained psychologist, but he knew when he was faced with someone who obviously was being guarded about something, a thing they didn't want to disclose. And Wilford looked to be afraid, the way he was drinking the liquor as though he needed to suppress a thought, a feeling, or a memory spoke volumes to Preston.

"Forgive me for prying, and it really is none of my business, but you do appear to be a little agitated. Is there anything wrong? Something I could help you with perhaps?" Wilford looked at Preston, his orange, thin hair neatly combed across an ever more revealing scalp, a neat fussy moustache that reminded Wilford of the whiskers worn by the actor Austin Trevor in his distinctive depiction of Hercule Poirot.

"Well, there is one thing, but I'm not sure what to make of it myself, and I'm afraid you might think me a foolish man if I were to tell you."

"Now you really have captured my curiosity! Shall I fetch us another round of drinks before you begin?" Wilford nodded, and Preston left the table for the bar. It couldn't hurt, Wilford thought, and perhaps talking about it would make it all seem so much more ordinary. When Preston returned, he set the two tumblers down, each containing a good-sized glug of Scotch over ice. Wilford took a sip of his and then began to talk about his singular experience at the place known locally as Wormbridge.

***

Wilford's travel timepiece woke him at seven in the morning. He sat up in bed and rubbed his temples. The previous night's drinking had brought him some 'carpenters in the forehead' this morning. Groaning, he turned back the bedsheets and climbed out of bed.

After dressing, and shaving, he made his way down to the bar. He used a telephone to contact his publisher, Phillip Letts. Letts was glad to hear from Wilford telling him that he had set up a radio programme at the BBC where it was hoped Wilford would perform a reading from his previous book of ghostly tales for the weekly show, *Appointment with Fear.*

Wilford was knocked for six at this news. According to Letts they originally wanted the distinguished character actor, Valentine Dyall, famous for his distinctive voice work on the BBC horror show. Dyall was unavailable, and Letts thought it would be a good blast if Wilford himself read from his own book. He said it would be a great publicity number and once his work had been broadcast on the radio the book sales would surely skyrocket. Reluctantly, Wilford agreed. The programme was to be broadcast tomorrow evening; however, there was still time for him to sort out what he had planned to do today.

During his talk with Preston the previous evening, it had been agreed that both men would journey along the cut towards Ulverstone. Wilford planned to take *Knotty Buoy* back to the Rose and Castle boat hire, where he hoped they could look into the problem he was having with the engine cutting out. Preston intended to go to Ulverstone to drop off some film to be developed at a chemist he used frequently, but he offered to travel first with Wilford to the winding hole where Wilford had seen the visions of the old Wormbridge tunnel.

Both men had arranged to meet after breakfast in the bar. When Wilford entered, he saw Preston already seated and finishing off a cup of coffee. Wilford greeted Preston, "Good morning, are you ready to set out?" Preston smiled and patted a small cloth bag that he had with him on the bar.

"Indeed, I have my films ready. I've taken quite a lot of pictures in the last couple of days. I wonder, did you take a look at my photograph, the one hanging on the staircase?" Wilford realised that he had meant to look but had forgotten to do so.

"Ah, no I'm afraid it slipped my mind, but we have time now if you'd like to show me." Preston was happy to see that Wilford was indeed showing an interest and he led the way to a position half way up the stairs. He pointed to a large photograph of the Portside Inn within a black and gold beaded wooden frame. The picture showed the front aspect of the Inn, and Preston had captured the light perfectly, the sunrise was visible across the upper windows of the Inn, and the water seemed to sparkle magically. "It's a very good picture, you are a talented photographer," said Wilford.

"Thank you! I took a few pictures of the Portside, for this one I used a long exposure as the light was dim, but unfortunately it has a flaw," confessed Preston. Wilford squinted slightly as he re-examined the photograph.

"Well it looks fine to me, but I wouldn't know what I was looking for." Preston pointed to a spot on the canal bank just to the right side of the Inn, where the lamppost stood.

"You see here?" he said and waited for Wilford to see what he had singled out. Wilford looked at the conical shaped opaque, and somewhat filamentous form that was half obscured by the stem of the lamppost.

"You mean this blotch?"

"Yes, it's a shame really. It must have been a person moving into frame. But I was sure there was nobody there when I set the camera on the tripod. It was very early in the morning." Wilford examined the blurred form more carefully.

"It does look like a person, possibly a woman, you see the skirt?" said Wilford.

"Yes, I thought it might have been the landlady, possibly she may have nipped outside for some reason or other. Anyway, I didn't want to keep it because I always notice the flaw. Rather than throw it away I thought it ought to hang here and Burt rather liked it." Wilford noticed that the ladylike smudge almost seemed to be staring right at the camera, although it was a subjective exercise to determine if a face could indeed be seen amongst the grey, ill-defined swirl.

***

Both Wilford and Preston were stood on the stern as Wilford guided *Knotty Buoy* along the cut towards Ulverstone. There was a knife-thin sheet of ice covering the water this morning, and the sound of the ice snapping and creaking accompanied them on their journey. The air was frozen but in stark contrast from the previous two days, it was free from the wind's laboured breath. Both men were glad of this as their faces were already chilled to the cheek bone.

When they approached the winding hole, Wilford gently steered the boat towards the far bank. He used the prickly bush that erupted from the border as a marker to line up the boat. When the boat was almost motionless in the water Wilford used a boathook to indicate where he had seen the illusory tunnel.

Preston followed the line of the hook but could only see an underbrush of thorn, and twig. There was no apparent semblance of any covert tunnel whatsoever.

Preston tried to reason with Wilford who stood adamant that they were indeed at the very place where he had described cruising along a tunnel lit by lantern light. "And you are firmly sure that this is the spot, that you couldn't have misplaced it? In the dark, in the fog?" Wilford shook his head,

"Here, look at the map," he handed both the old map and a newer version to Preston, "there are no other divergences along this stretch leading to Ulverstone. The only junction that ever existed and once cut off from this bank was the old Wormbridge underpass." Preston studied the maps as Wilford kept the boat steady in the water.

"I see what you mean. Unless you had travelled some considerable distance away from Ulverstone and judging by the scale on this map, the next junction is some twenty-four miles or so and would place you at Log's Bank, near Merewich."

"Well I can assure you I didn't go that far, I would have known, and besides, there are locks to go through and the junction at Log's Bank doesn't appear to show a tunnel, bridge, or anything." Preston looked again at the maps,

"I really don't understand what could have happened. I hoped somehow that I would find the answer, but I haven't been much help at all." Preston handed both maps back to Wilford as he peered deep into the thicket next to them. He noticed the same piles of broken bricks Wilford had spotted earlier, some of them half buried in the bankside. He rubbed his forehead and let out a long sigh. "But if you are adamant," he watched as Wilford nodded signifying that he was.

Preston used the boathook to grasp a clump of interwoven thorny branches. He pulled on the hook bringing the brushwood close to them. He asked Wilford to hold the boathook whilst he took a white handkerchief out of his trouser pocket and he tied the handkerchief to a stout twig. When the hook was released the thorns snapped back to their original position. "Well at least now you have a marker. If you should ever be lost on the water in the fog and unclear about where you are, and if you should see that tunnel of yours, you can look for the handkerchief. If it's not tied to the bush, then you can't be here." It was such a simple solution Wilford laughed out loud,

"Why I didn't think of this I'll never know," he said.

Preston was dropped off near Ulverstone, he said he would catch a bus back to the inn.

Wilford then travelled to the Rose and Castle boat hire and he moored *Knotty Buoy*.

Wilford had found Howard Durnsten out amongst his boats, he had his Labrador, Jess with him. Jess came bouncing over to greet Wilford who gave him a fuss. He explained the issues he had been having with the engine to Howard who asked him to wait at the boathouse where he said Mrs Durnsten would fix him up with a cuppa, and if he was in luck, a slice of her famous fruit loaf. Howard said he would have a look over the boat to see if he could spot anything that might be amiss.

There was a cheery fire in the grate at the boathouse. Wilford sat waiting for Howard to return from *Knotty Buoy*. As anticipated, Mrs Durnsten had provided him with a mug of tea and a thick slice of buttered fruit loaf.

As he sat, eating his fruit loaf, he tried several times to make light conversation with Mrs Durnsten, but it was hard work. She seemed not to want to talk with him. She said it was her ears, claiming her hearing was not as good as it once was. Wilford remembered last time he was at the boathouse, when he mentioned to the Durnstens that he was here to carry out some research on the stories of *Aggie* for his new book. The reception turned colder after that, from Mrs Durnsten at least.

Howard Durnsten returned to the boathouse hanging his bowler off a long hat peg. He stood in front of the fire with his hands outstretched, "Cor, blummin' cold out today," he uttered. Wilford asked if he had found anything wrong with *Knotty Buoy*. "Nothing I could see. Engine seemed fine. You said the engine keeps cutting off?" Wilford nodded. "Could be the isolation switches, or something jamming the propeller," added Howard.

"The horn seems to be faulty too," remembered Wilford.

"The horn? That's odd, it's a new horn, fitted it myself. It might be some water ingress." Howard was handed a mug of tea by his wife, he slurped as he continued to ponder all the possibilities.

"Yes, I was on the cut in the dark you see, the engine died and so did the lamps. I almost had a collision with another boat. I couldn't sound the trumpet to warn them. They weren't happy with me I can tell you."

"Sorry to hear about all this sir. I would take him in to the Bell, see what Malcom could make of it. I know a lot about boats, but what Malcom Renshaw doesn't know, nobody does." As Howard spoke of the Bell boatyard Mrs Durnsten began to cough and fidget in her chair by the fire. "Thing is sir, the Bell's closed for business on account of a family bereavement." Wilford stood up on hearing this news.

"Oh, what happened? I was only at the boatyard yesterday."

"Malcom's younger brother Harry, he was found dead last night," answered Howard. Wilford was shocked at the news having only met and spoke with Harry the previous day.

"I can hardly believe it," he said.

"Did you know the man?" asked Howard.

"Well not exactly. I went there to talk to him about an incident that he'd been involved with, out on the water. It was reported in the local paper. He seemed fine when we talked, a little soused with liquor I'll admit, but nothing indicating him being in ill health. What happened?"

"An accident sir, or so it seems. He was found drowned, with his foot snagged on a mooring rope. His brother found him, said the eels had been at his eyes already. Not a pretty business they say. Word travels fast round here sir." As Howard finished speaking his wife fussed and shook her head. She could certainly hear what Howard was saying mused Wilford.

"Well I'm truly shocked!" said Wilford. "Next time you see Malcom please give him my condolences." Howard nodded.

"I will sir. Now back to the matter of *Knotty Buoy*, if you leave him with me for today, I'll give him a thorough going over. Should be ready to pick up, say around four to five this afternoon. Unless there's a serious problem. If that's the case I can fix you up with a replacement." Wilford agreed that it all sounded like a good plan. He told Howard he had some business in London, and if there was a problem with the engine, he was happy to leave it here for servicing until he got back.

Before Wilford left the boathouse, he asked if Howard could provide some directions to Damdike Bank.

"Damdike Bank?" said Howard aghast, "what business would you 'ave up at Damdike Bank, only nothing much up there is all?"

"I need to speak with someone before I head off to London, in fact it was poor Harry Renshaw who suggested-" Mrs Durnsten suddenly cut in the conversation,

"Only person lives up Damdike Bank is Elsie Hardwicke. She's an old woman. She don't need no badgering." Howard looked to be a little embarrassed about his wife's sudden outburst.

"I only want a couple of minutes of her time," explained Wilford, "and I am willing to pay her for it. It's just that I need to hear from her, about the old days, for my book." Howard showed Wilford to the door and they both stepped outside. The air was biting cold.

"Please sir, don't mind Mrs Durnsten, she be like the other folks around the place. They don't like no stirrin' up mucky waters, if you take my meaning."

"Like I said, I have to get ready to catch a train to London later, I only want a quick word, she may not even see me, perhaps she's not in."

"Oh, she'll be in alright. Elsie seldom leaves the cottage. Her eldest daughter looks after her now, so it's Mary you'll have to see first." Durnsten gave Wilford some general directions and Wilford thanked him before making his way along the canal bank towards Damdike.

***

Wilford passed a white, metal, painted sign post with *Damdike Bank* embossed in bold black lettering. With only one dwelling standing by the canal it was a safe bet to assume that it was Elsie's cottage.

The cottage was built from a pale stock brick, it had a slated gabled roof; was only single story and the façade sported five irregular sized windows that faced the canal. A small timber porch complete with slate pinnacle roof framed the front door. Nailed to the porch was a metal sign that read: '*Keeper's cottage.*' The door itself sported a cast iron doorknocker in the shape of a swan.

Wilford rapped on the door using the swan and after waiting a short time the door was opened by a short, stout, grey-haired woman wearing an oversized, knitted red sweater, and a long blue skirt. She was drying her hands with a tea towel as she stood in the doorway, "Mrs Elsie Hardwicke?" enquired Wilford. The woman shook her head,

"No, that's my mother, you must be the new doctor, come in," she said as she stepped aside allowing Wilford to enter. Inside, the house was simply furnished, there was a musty smell about the place.

"You must be Mary," spoke Wilford.

"Aye, I am. Did you bring the cough syrup? Only she's been hackin' all neet!" Wilford thought it best to clear up the confusion over his own identity,

"My name is Wilford Bailey, I'm not the doctor I'm afraid." Mary stared at him,

"Oh, what do you want with my mother then?"

"I'm a writer, from Oxford. I would like to speak with your mother if I may. You see, I'm collecting old stories and accounts of life on the waterways, for a book. I was told your mother, with all her local knowledge, could help me. I'm willing to pay for her time." Wilford pulled some ten shilling notes out from his wallet for Mary to see. Mary took the money from his hand and put it in one of her skirt pockets,

"Can't see the harm of it. You'll find her through there," she pointed towards a half open green door, "she might be tired though, like I said, she was up all neet hackin'."

Wilford found Elsie sat in a somewhat shabby armchair angled to face a small coal fire. She had her milk white hair wrapped in a tight bun. A black shawl covered her shoulders. Yellow flames skipped across black coals and cast a warm glow to liven her wizened features. He carried a wooden ladderback chair over to where she sat mesmerised by the flames as though reading them. He set the chair down to face her. He coughed politely to steal her attention.

"Oh, you got it too have you?" she said as she fixed him with a kindly stare. He noticed how the firelight reflected from her watery eyes; he could see a reflection of the burnished copper kettle that was hanging over the fire itself. Elsie used her leathery hands to pull the shawl tight about her shoulders. "Have you brought me cough syrup?" she asked before she launched into a staccato round of coughing almost akin to the manner of a Gatling gun.

"Sorry, I'm not a doctor, but your cough seems very bad. Is there anything I can do for you whilst I'm here?" asked Wilford after noticing how sick she appeared. Elsie used a hand to wave him away,

"Oh, it's not the cough that carries you off, it's the coffin they carry you offin," she replied chuckling slightly before a further round of spluttering. "That new doctor Renley, waiting for him to turn up is like waiting to be hung.

Mind you, the old one had a face like a farmer's arse on a frosty morning!" Wilford smiled at Elsie as she repositioned herself in her chair before asking who in fact he was, and what business he had with her. He explained about his books, and how it was Harry Renshaw who guided him here.

Elsie fussed when she learned from Wilford about Harry's recent tragic accident. "An accident they said did they, dear, dear. Such a good boy he was. A useful boy to his mother." She glanced at the mantle clock, "Oh me eyes, how much is the clock young man?" she asked. Wilford realising that she meant to know the time told her it was eleven o'clock. "Doctor should have been here by now, oh he's about as much use as toothache." Wilford thought that it was as good a time as any to begin to ask Elsie about what she knew about *Aggie*.

The first thing she told Wilford was that it was a dangerous business he was getting into. There had been many deaths over the years, and in spite of what the authorities said regarding circumstance and facts leading up to the deaths, the people around Ulverstone believed in their hearts that there was more to the deaths than could be explained away by misfortunate accidents.

Elsie told Wilford to be careful who he talked to. Not everyone took kindly to strangers whisking up old feelings and awakening old worries.

Wilford asked Elsie what he had been desperate to know all along. Who was *Aggie*, and what had happened all those years ago? Now, Elsie liked a good old chin wag, especially since becoming housebound in recent years. She could talk till the cows came home, and she never got to see anyone no more, except Mary, and the local doctor. She was more than happy to chat about the old days, besides, this pleasant young man had a polite demeanour. Wilford took out his notebook and pencil and sat back by the crackling fire in anticipation of some much-needed answers.

Five

"I must have been nothing but a wee slip of a girl back in them days. Barely out of terry towelling," began Elsie. "I was one of the few lucky ones to have a school to go to. When I say school, well, it was nothing like folks call school nowadays, oh no. It was run by the local parish in Ulverstone, or *'Ullerstone'* as we called it then.

Aye, I was lucky to have schooling, however basic it was. Most kids in *Ullerstone* were sent out to work, to make money for their families. Oh yes, times were hard back then. I dare say a bright young man like you would find it hard to imagine." Wilford smiled but said nothing, allowing Elsie to continue with her accounts from her childhood.

"I was lucky, you see my father earned enough to allow me to have an education of sorts, just up to the age of ten though I must add. But back in them days, that was the usual way.

Aye, a quiet girl she was. Pretty as a picture, people said. A quiet girl. My head is all full of hornswoggle these days, but I think I can remember her name," Elsie sat a while pondering as she watched the fire. "Ah, yes. Coco. Coco Darcel. She had slightly swarthy looks, beautiful dark hair that shone like silk. Image of her mother she was.

We were not close friends mind, but we played and chatted on occasion, as youngsters do. We often played out on the meadow near the schoolhouse. She always had a ragdoll under her arm and wouldn't go anyplace without it. I remember the times we picked sun red apples from a thick gnarled-up old apple tree.

My old gran said that tree had stood near the schoolhouse for so long that all the history from the soggy earth from which it grew had been all soaked up and pushed into the apples that bunched from its boughs.

We used to fill our skirts with apples, carrying them down to the cut. We'd collect up feathers from rooks and ducks and push them into the tops where the stalks grew. We'd chuck them in the water and watch them sail along the cut like little fat boats. The rest we'd eat until our bellies ached.

People always said that there was something of the gypsy in Coco, and they were right. Coco's mother Maggie, or Aggie as she became known, was descended from gypsy stock. There was no doubt about that. She lived with Henry Darcel, a local lockkeeper of the time, they told others that they were married. My ma told me that they were just shacked up together, living o'er the broom as it were, probably couldn't afford to get wed proper like.

That Henry Darcel was no catch mind, face like Humpty Dumpty, and bow-legged. He couldn't stop a pig in a ginnel! He was always in a sour mood and could start an argument in an empty room. He didn't mind using his fists on a woman either. Everyone felt sorry for Aggie. There was always talk about the town that Aggie had a secret love, one of the gypsies over near Damdike Bank.

The talk was sometimes too slack for comfort, and this spurred Henry to suspect that his daughter Coco, was not his own flesh and blood. To be honest, we all doubted it."

Elsie's mood seemed to change, she looked troubled, saddened by the memories that were now being slowly rekindled in the embers of her mind. "I remember the day when Coco didn't show at school. I thought it was all the apples we ate two evenings before. I Thought it had made her belly sour enough to keep her at home, but I was wrong, so very wrong.

The first moment I suspected something wasn't right was when my ma came to meet me after the school bell had rung out. There she was waiting, her face all red from crying. Her eyes all sore and puffy. Before I could ask, what the matter be, she gripped me so tight and we both stood there hugging and hugging till I could hardly breathe. I wasn't the only one to be collected by their ma, or da that day either. The whole village seemed to be waiting outside the schoolhouse.

When I got home my ma told me what had happened. Little Coco never came home from school the previous day. Her ma, Aggie, had spent the whole night looking. Henry and most of the men from the village searched everywhere but there was no trace.

Aggie continued to look for her little girl even when everyone else had given up. She walked the cut by day and night carrying her lantern as the searched and called for Coco. She would go banging on the door of the Otter and the Portside Inn begging the men to go out looking with her, but they were too full of ale and pie to care. Most thought they'd done their share of searching, and that it was now a lost cause. Even the Bobbies had given up.

We all knew that Coco was never coming back the day the canals were dredged and even though her body wasn't found by the dredging. It didn't seem real to me, I was only a girl and death was something else, something so very far away. I could still see Coco, clear as day in my mind. I could still hear her in my thoughts, her laughter as we played on the cut, the girl with the doll tucked tightly under her arm, our apples bobbing along, dividing the ducks as they swam past. It didn't seem real that she was dead and that I'd never see her again.

Aggie pleaded with every boater who sailed the cut to take her with them, to search with her for her little girl. None of them paid her no mind, thinking she was just a crazy old woman with a thirst for gin. She was not a day over thirty-six, but grief had aged her. She'd given up eating. She was so thin, what clothes she still wore hung off her like old coal sacks, and her hair, once dark, and silky was now grey and jumbled.

I was out walking with my ma one day when we saw her, she was carrying her lantern, swaying as though she'd taken too much grog, but it was the lack of food and sleep that made her roll on and off the bricks of Wormbridge tunnel. I remember my ma saying, 'Goodness, is that poor Aggie? She looks like she's bin dragged thru' bushes backwards,' and that was the last time I saw her, as a woman, but we'll come to that later."

Elsie stopped talking and began a series of coughing spurts that at times became so violent Wilford was forced to fetch Mary. After

Mary had settled her and made her a hot toddy, she was ready to continue her story.

"Henry, at this point had shut Aggie out of the family home. He told everyone who asked that she had gone plain mad and although it had been a terrible loss they had both suffered, a tragedy of the worst kind, he had decided to get on with his life, he had a job to do and people depended on him to do it, and he couldn't do it with Aggie in her state hanging around the place.

Henry had now started openly accusing her of being unfaithful, accusing her of bedding with Manfri, a gypsy from up near Damdike. He told Aggie to go to him, but Manfri denied all knowledge of Aggie not that she cared at this point, nobody had even heard her speak other than to shout the name of her child as she searched day and night by a lantern's light.

The story went that Aggie overheard Henry as he stood one windy night, pickled in ale outside the Otter. He was drinking with some of his boater friends and was boasting, telling them how he'd rid himself of an unfaithful wife and a bastard child.

She came at him all teeth and nails, but he sent her, with his boot, for a ducking in the cut, and the water that night was as cold as the northside of a January gravestone. She must have dragged herself out of the water and made her way back to what used to be her home because they say she found Coco's doll, half buried under a heap of coal along with Coco's dress, the dress she had been wearing the night she never came home. The doll and dress were covered in dried blood according to what the Bobbies said back in the day. Aggie posted a note through the door of St. Mary's Parish telling what she had found before she went back to the Otter.

Aggie must have known a man would be hung for doing what he'd done to a child. The law of the land was one in which murderers paid the highest price. But Aggie didn't need no Bobbies, or no law men to give her the justice she wanted. An eye for an eye, the law according to a mother's revenge was all the justice she needed. And by all accounts, she got just that.

She found Henry snoring like a train, laid out on a bunk in his boat and still moored on the bank of the Otter. She'd tied him to his bunk using some loose mooring ropes she found on the deck. He was probably so drunk to know what she was doing. She finally tipped lamp oil all over him and everywhere inside the cabin before tossing her own lantern inside the boat.

According to the landlord and landlady of the Otter, Aggie just sat on the bank laughing like a Tomfool whilst the boat burned like a tinder haystack. Folks from the Otter came rushing down to try to fight the fire using buckets that they filled from the cut, but nothing could be done. According to some they could hear Henry screaming so loudly the noise could peel the skin off a pair of ears.

Aggie quietly sank beneath the waters at Wormbridge that night whilst men at the Otter got their lungs scorched fighting a floating bonfire. She simply drowned herself. Maybe she thought it was the only way she could be reunited with her Coco. The next day, a boater found her face down in the water, caught up in a floating island of weeds and old bottles. They say when they fished her out, she was still clutching Coco's doll.

They buried Aggie in the churchyard at St Mary on the hill. There was nothing left of Henry to bury. They found the lifeless body of poor little Coco sometime later, she was stuffed inside an old hollow tree not thirty yards from the cottage where she'd lived. They said she'd been strangled, but there was some confusion about that far as I recall. At the funeral they put her doll in with her and laid her to rest next to her mother. They say the gypsies paid for the gravestone. Maybe one of them had a heavy conscience. Like I said, some folks thought that there was something of the gypsy about Aggie, and there are some who believe in the gypsy hex.

There were some who heard Aggie cuss and curse the whole town when she sat there, screaming and hollering whilst Henry burned like a tallow candle. What happened exactly to Coco we shall never know, and it's best we don't know. I can only imagine the terrible wicked deed and how that little girl must have suffered. The whole business left a scar on the town that's never healed to this day. All folks born here since, are somehow stained by the badness and dirt in the muck and water. It's like what my old gran said about them apples on that old tree, all that history, all those echoes growing inside each and every one of us.

No doubt you've seen the boats with the dollies tied to the fenders?" Wilford nodded that he had seen them, but he didn't disclose the fact that he'd purchased one of his own. "People believe that Aggie will leave them be if they decorate their boat with one of the dollies, because it tells Aggie that they mourn as she mourns for the loss of her little girl. But it doesn't do any good, no. Aggie will never rest until the cut runs dry, until all the blood has run out of this town, until the town itself is taken over by tree and bramble. A revenge of a different sort by a different mother, that of Mother Nature."

Wilford allowed Elsie to have a respite from her tales whilst she ate some stew that Mary had brought her. Wilford also accepted some of the warm lunch together with a piece of bread. He was grateful to hear about the background to Aggie, whether this was a true account or not he had no way of knowing seeing as Elsie was probably the only person alive today who had been around back then.

Wilford knew from what Harry Renshaw had told him that Elsie was herself a witness to an actual encounter with Aggie. It was this account he was hoping to hear about next. When Elsie had set her empty bowl down by the hearth Wilford began to ask her about her own experience with Aggie.

Elsie looked Wilford in the eye and then spoke, "I know you must think me a mad old duck, but I don't lie young man, lying is listed as a sin in the Ten Commandments." Wilford assured Elsie that he didn't think of her as prone to telling fibs. She settled back in her chair, pulling at her shawl again prompting Wilford to empty the coal scuttle into the grate. Soon the fire was reawakened and became so hot that the pair of them had to push themselves back from its blaze.

"We all feared being on the water back then, but we had jobs to do and we had to get on with it. We all heard ... things. Everyone had a tale to tell, but never from the lips of the living.

It was a hot summer that was. I grew tall for a girl of twelve I did, although you wouldn't think that to look at me now, all bent and old I am, with a back like the bight of an elbow. But I was tall, and quite strong. My uncle Alf, he used to borra my dad's boat when it wasn't needed, and he'd use it to shift some goods for the warehouses along the old *Ullerstone* cut. He was kind of freelance.

One day Alf asked if I could help him on the boat, me not having any brothers and Alf wasn't married and had no kids to speak of either. I was offered three shilling and ninepence, not bad for a girl.

We loaded up the boat with spun cloth from a local woollen mill. The journey to Macclesfield would take us a day or more. We were barely out of *Ullerstone* and on the cut near Wormbridge when the boat stopped dead in the water.

I still remember how strange it all seemed. The birds had stopped singing, the wind rustling through the trees seemed to pause like as if I'd put my hands up over my ears. Only ... I hadn't.

I remember Uncle Alf panic-stricken as he raced around the boat, his eyes like hard boiled eggs, starin' like he was in fear for his life. I didn't realise it right away, but that's just what he was. Scared, so scared I saw a small yellow river flood out from the bottom of his pant leg.

Alf grabbed me and told me to swim to the bank, he said he'd seen something in the water, and it looked like merry hell! Well I thought that if he'd seen something in the water, something bad, bad enough to stop a barge weighing many tons, then I sure as heck wasn't throwing myself in it. But in the end, that's just what I did do.

The banging started, banging like someone had taken a hammer to the underside of the hull. We both went below deck and I saw something I'll never forget till the good lord sees fit to ease my suffering and takes me off this earth for good.

The hull was broke inwards and upwards. There was a big old whirlpool of bubbling water as the splintered deck planks were pushed up through the hole. Alf was screaming as the barge was flooding, '*Git offer her Elsie, git off,*' he cried. And then I saw it, or her I should say. Two great hands; long swollen fingers with curled nails like billhooks. Both hands were flapping about in the spouting, gurgling brown water. '*Git off Elsie, Aggie will have us, save yourself,*' were the last words I heard my Uncle Alf say.

I ran up top deck, the barge was already tippin' by then. I jumped in the cut and swam for my life. As I swam to the bank all I could think of was how scared Alf's face was as those bloated white hands reached out for him and dragged him through the hull.

When I reached the bank, I was dragged out by two men who'd seen our boat in trouble. I pleaded with them to help my uncle, neither of them went in after him, both just took off their hats and pressed them to their chests and bowed their heads. I remember thinking, why are you not going to do anything? I tried to go back in myself, but they stopped me, they dragged me away sobbing my heart out. I carried on sobbing until I had no more strength to even breathe proper.

I don't know why I survived when so many others have fallen, whether be by accident or sickness, she'll always find a way. Perhaps it was because I was Coco's friend. Maybe that's why. I often wonder."

Elsie appeared to have come to the end of her story. Wilford watched as she sat silent, in deep thought, watching the fire's burning fingers reaching upwards to claw at smouldering fire brick and soot-lined flue. It was as though the flames were reminding her with scorching visions of the past, visions that have been branded into her memory and have kept her awake at night for almost eighty years.

Wilford asked Elsie a question, "Do you really believe Aggie is still here, that she still acts out her revenge on those who sail the canals and rivers of Ulverstone?" Elsie nodded,

"She is as constant as the wind, or the rain. As long as there is an Ulverstone, Aggie will be part of it." Wilford then asked her a burning question,

"Do you believe that anyone who somehow gets too close to Aggie, even in some small way. Can they be harmed?" Elsie looked at Wilford, she looked deep into his brown eyes, and then her own grey, creamy eyes widened enough to iron out the wrinkles that had cut rivulets deep down into her cheeks,

"Oh, you poor boy," she said. Wilford smiled a nervous smile, and that smile gave away a dozen secrets to Elsie Hardwicke.

"I'm sorry, I'm not sure what you-"

"Take my advice young man. Leave this town and never come back. Go today, don't waste time." Elsie became more animated. That shrivelled, drowsy, ancient woman only moments before now standing almost to her once full height, and Wilford did note, that she was indeed tall for a girl.

"Go home, back to Oxford or wherever it was you said you came from. You'll be safe in Oxford." Wilford stood aghast,

"It's just that I've ... seen things, when I've been out on my boat." He felt foolish for telling her, but he was so afraid that he might be suffering the first signs of dementia. Anything she could tell him, no matter how fanciful, how ludicrous it might be, was a blessing if it helped point a path away from mental sickness. He needed to hear it. It was easier and more relieving to believe in *Aggie*.

"Seen things? What 'ave you seen boy? Things stirrin' in the water? Lights?" He would have told Elsie everything, if Mary had not come into the room. He may have even blabbed like a loon about the charred boat that had encased the most haunted screams that he had ever heard. Mary grew concerned when she had heard her mother becoming more enlivened.

Mary explained to Wilford that her mother had had enough excitement for one day, which Elsie brushed off by telling Mary not to be so daft. "Nevertheless," said Mary, "I think my mother needs some rest," she was adamant that Wilford should now leave. Elsie sat herself down again next to the fire,

"Oh, we all would live a long time, but none wants to be old," Elsie added, "Remember, stay away from the lights. They're set to draw in folk, to keep them with her. Once you follow the lights and linger, you may become stuck. No way back for them as be stuck. Cut your lights out and leave your liver int' dark she will."

Wilford thanked both Elsie and Mary for their time. As he left the cottage, he could still hear Elsie as she rambled on about how Wilford should get on a train back to Oxford and forget about his stories and his foolish book. As he walked up high on the bank at Damdike he could see the spire of the church of St. Mary on the hill. As he was only a ten-minute walk or less from the church, he decided to pay it a visit to see if Elsie's story was corroborated by evidence of a burial for

Aggie and Coco. He liked to use a mixture of anecdotal and factual evidence in his books.

Even though it was only early afternoon, the daylight was struggling to hold back the oncoming dusk and the crows had already begun to roost. Wilford walked along a thin and winding pea-shingle path which led all the way around the churchyard. He stopped briefly to read the inscriptions on some of the grave markers, but he couldn't see any extoled with the names *Aggie*, or *Coco*.

He bent down to straighten a small impish cherub that at some time had been knocked over so that its lichen encrusted granite face; perpetually frozen in an overwrought grimace, was now leaning against the towering gravestone alongside. He read the inscription that was eulogising some time-lost lord of a manor, a squire of Ulverstone.

The gravestone and much of the grave had become concealed by a tangled mess of last summer's stickeljack and wild grass. He began to clear it away using a gloved hand when a voice rang out from behind, "Not a relative of yours surely?" Wilford turned to see a man not all that older than he was, he wore the apparel of a vicar complete with collar and gown.

Wilford stood and greeted the vicar who introduced himself as the reverend Mathew Fell. "No, not one of mine. I *was* looking for a grave as it happens. I wonder if you would be able to help me find it."

"I will try my best, although I don't have all that much time," spoke the reverend, "you see I was about to leave on an errand. Do you have a name for it?"

"Maggie, or perhaps Aggie. I don't have a surname, but maybe Darcel?" replied Wilford. The reverend nodded,

"Yes, I know of it, but I think you might be a little disappointed." The reverend asked Wilford to follow him as he led him over to where a large, somewhat dead holly bush sprouted. At the base of the bush, there was a jagged, angular piece of rock. "I'm afraid that's all that remains of it. It used to stand almost three feet tall, or so I believe. I never saw it whole." Wilford couldn't see any inscription. As he brushed away a layer of sloughed crisp holly leaves, he thought about the old superstition of how a holly bush, or any thorny shrub for that matter was thought to be able to entangle a spirit, trapping it on earth.

"What happened to the stone?" asked Wilford.

"Well, I don't believe in ghost stories Mr Bailey, but the locals seem to be gripped particularly by this one I hear. The grave was destroyed a long time ago I believe. Someone who took a disliking to it tried to remove it using a sledge hammer. As you were searching for it, I imagine you are already familiar with the stories concerning it."

"Indeed. I should have said, I'm a writer by profession, and I came to Ulverstone to research some local tales of the haunting of these waterways by Aggie."

"Oh yes, the grey lady with the lamp, who walks the riverbanks in search of her lost daughter, tipping the boats and sending the occupants to a watery grave. Yes, I have heard all the stories." Wilford stood from his kneeling position near the graveside,

"Well I'd hoped to read the inscription, so I could put it into my book and see if there was any truth in all the names that have been added to this renowned legend."

"I might still be able to help you there," said the reverend happily, "there is a register of all the burials at St. Mary. The book itself dates to the seventeenth century. I can write it all down for you." Wilford was pleased at this news.

"I would be most grateful if you could do that for me."

"It would be no trouble, but like I said, I was about to go on an errand so perhaps I could send it on to you. Are you staying somewhere local?"

"Yes, the Portside Inn."

"I know it, I shall send a copy of what's written in the book. Perhaps you could send me a copy of your book when it's finished? I would much like to read it." Wilford handed the reverend one of his cards so that he'd remember who to send the information to.

$\mathscr{Six}$

W ilford was back in his room at the Portside Inn. He had booked himself a taxi to take him to the train station near Ulverstone. It was almost Five in the afternoon and the taxi was booked for five thirty.

After leaving the Church of St. Mary on the hill, he had returned to the Rose and Castle boat hire yard. Howard Durnsten told him that he thought he'd discovered the reason for *Knotty Buoy's* engine operating so erratically. He asked Wilford to take it in to the Bell boatyard when he was back from London. They had the only spare part for miles around that would fit, and they had offered to do the work for Durnsten.

Now seated in front of his typewriter, he was typing out a note he was going to ask Burt's son-in-law to deliver to Corinne for him; he still hadn't acquired the number of the room she was staying in. The note explained that he had been asked to record a radio programme tomorrow evening in London and that he would have to break their dinner date. He had apologised quite earnestly saying that he would like to rearrange their dinner as soon as he returned.

He wondered if he should have written the note in his own hand, so that it appeared more personal; however, his handwriting was rather untidy. He didn't wish for her to misread the note and have its meaning misconstrued. He folded the note and popped it into an envelope, and he wrote 'Corinne' on the front before packing a suitcase and making his way down to the bar.

Wilford introduced himself to John properly this time as he handed him the note. John explained that he was not too familiar with all the guests who were staying at the Inn yet but said he would find out Corinne's room number and hand her the note. Wilford then asked John if he would mind keeping an eye on *Knotty Buoy* as he intended to leave the boat moored outside the Inn until he returned from London. "Which boat would that be sir?" John asked as he peered out through the windows,

"The one moored near the lamppost. It's the only one." John frowned then rubbed his eyes,

"Forgive me sir, but for a moment I thought there were two boats by the lamppost ... I must have been mistaken," he said with a perplexed glance back towards the window. Wilford himself glanced out through the window and saw *Knotty Buoy* moored alone and bobbing rhythmically upon the water.

He thanked John and was about to leave the Inn to wait outside for the imminent arrival of his taxi when he saw Corinne sitting at a familiar table near the window. He asked John for the note back and quickly made his way over to her, he was wearing a broad smile.

Corinne seemed happy to see him, and greeted him with a beaming smile of her own, then she frowned, "Oh dear, have I got my days muddled up?" she asked him, "were we to have dinner tonight? I was sure it was arranged for Thursday," she said contritely.

"No need to apologise Corinne, you're not wrong. We did arrange to have dinner tomorrow, but I'm afraid I'll have to break our date, you see, I've been asked to go to London, to do a radio show. Thing is, it's tomorrow evening. I'm so sorry really."

"That sounds exciting. Please don't worry, we can have dinner another time." Wilford handed her the note.

"I wrote you a letter, explaining. But no need for it now, I guess. You're sure you don't mind?"

"Not at all. Please, tell me when is the show on air? I'd like to tune in if you don't mind." Wilford placed the note down in front of Corinne. She picked it up. Over at the bar, John stood drying a glass with a towel, he studied Wilford as he talked with Corinne.

"To be honest, I've never done anything like this before. Radio broadcasting is a first for me and I'm really quite nervous."

"I'm sure you'll be smashing. Has it got something to do with your ghost book?"

"Yes, a promotional thing. My publisher, Phillip, he seems to think it will be a good blast. It should be going out tomorrow about eight in the evening."

"I shall definitely remember Wilford, I shall listen with mother. She enjoys a good story." Corinne looked down at Wilford's suitcase, "I must be holding you up. You should be going surely?" He looked into Corinne's clear blue eyes, he thought how much they shone like crystal gemstones, the light from inside the Inn even seemed to refract off them as though they were faceted.

He wanted to pick up the telephone at once and call Phillip. He wanted to tell him that he wasn't coming to London to do the blasted radio show. He wanted to take Corinne by the hand and leave the Inn where they would ride a taxi into town, discover a nice, quiet, almost private little bistro. They would eat delicious food, drink intoxicating wine, clasp hands as a waiter lights a solitary candle for them whilst they gaze into each other's eyes, discovering more about each other and feeling giddy like children. Alas, he felt obligated to participate in the broadcast.

Wilford said goodbye to Corinne when he saw the taxi pull up outside. The luminous taxi top sign burned brightly on the gravel drive near the Inn. Soon Wilford was seated inside with his suitcase stowed safely away in the boot of the vehicle.

As the taxi reversed then straightened enabling the driver to head out to town, Wilford dragged a finger down the window to clear away a patch of condensation that had steadily built up inside the car due to the inclement weather outside. He saw Corinne as she sat by the window, her face slightly rippled and distorted into solemnity by the waves in the aged glass panes.

***

The journey to London lasted a good five and a half hours. Wilford wiled away the time by reading the ghost story that he was expected to perform the following evening. The story was from his second book of urban ghost stories and Phillip had chosen it as one of the best and most suitable to the style of the radio series.

After reading the story for the umpteenth time, his eyes grew heavy and he catnapped for a while until the loud shrill blast of the locomotive air whistle dragged him from the clutches of Morpheus. The train was pulling into King's Cross station.

Taking the underground to Great Portland Street station via St. Pancras, Wilford eventually reached the Manvellian hotel where he would be staying for two nights. A far cry from the Portside Inn, the Manvellian was a rather luxurious hotel and only just over a third of a mile from BBC Broadcasting House.

Wilford decided that he would hit the hay as soon as he had taken a quick bath. It was almost eleven at night when he had checked into the hotel. He knew his meeting with Phillip wasn't until lunchtime, but he wanted to feel fresh as he embarked on his nerve-racking first experience of radio performance.

Wilford had hoped to sleep like a top. He didn't. His mind was troubled by his recent experiences whilst exploring Ulverstone and his fears that he was somehow losing his senses and was walking down a path of hereditary senescence. His travel timepiece rang out with its sonorous tinkling bell, but he had in truth been lying awake for many hours.

***

145

Wilford and Phillip met for lunch in a café on Portland Place. They had discussed the format of the radio broadcast in that it would form part of the horror drama series, *Appointment with Fear*. The format would comprise a reading of a chosen ghost story with the title: *When the babes sleep*, a tale chronicled by Wilford after spending time in Tiptree where he interviewed a middle-aged woman who had responded to his advert in the *Sketch magazine* asking for true ghost stories.

The remainder of the show would be taken up by a brief dramatization of part of a W. W. Jacobs story acted by the in-house team of performers. Wilford was happy that the section in which he was involved was only short, a mere ten or so minutes long.

After their meal Wilford and Phillip parted company. Phillip made his way over to Broadcasting house whilst Wilford took a stroll down Oxford street. He spent some time perusing the many shops and even making a few purchases; however, only small items as he was ever mindful that he had to carry it all back with him to Ulverstone the next day. Finally, he made his way back to the hotel where he successfully caught an hour or so of much needed sleep before he dressed and set out to BBC Broadcasting house by foot.

Wilford had never been to Broadcasting house or even seen the building before. He stood gazing upwards at the edifice of Portland stone elegantly presented in an Art Deco style. Over the front entrance stood a sculpture in the form of two statues, Prospero and Ariel, both taken from the play: *The Tempest* by William Shakespear.

He thought that the choice of Ariel, being the *'spirit of the air'*, was apt for an organisation that had taken the pathway of transmitting through the airwaves. The whole business of broadcasting was still something of a mystery to him, and as he pondered on the many questions surrounding radio, he stepped inside the building.

Wilford was met by Phillip who took him to a waiting area on the sixth floor where he was also greeted by members of the production crew for the broadcast. After some blithe greetings, he was presented with a handful of papers clipped together. He cast an eye over them and realised they were typed pages of the story he was scheduled to read. Phillip came over to Wilford when he saw him frowning at the papers, "Anything wrong old boy?" Phillip asked whilst packing fresh tobacco into his walnut pipe.

"Not really, only that this isn't exactly how I wrote it. And I practiced it the way it was in the book." Phillip lit his pipe and took the pages from Wilford's hands,

"Colin's the chap who sorts these things out." Phillip waved over at Colin, writer and producer of the series. He came over to see them. He was a tall thin man with heavy spectacles and receding greying hair, he wore a grey woollen cardigan over a blue shirt open at the neck to reveal a paisley cravat. "Say Colin, my man here says the story's been changed. Is he right?" Colin lifted the papers from Philip and briefly studied the contents.

"Yes, just for phonetics, and to avoid any unnecessary tongue-twisters. I thought some of the expressions may cause a problem when read. We have done this sort of thing before you know. It will be much easier for you to read aloud now we've tinkered with it, but we haven't changed any of the essence of the story." Colin thrust the papers back into Wilford's hands who nodded his understanding and quickly put all the papers back in the correct order. "I think they are about to start," said Phillip and he tapped Wilford on the shoulder, "but don't worry, it's not going out live. They'll record it all first, then pipe it out later if all's good." Wilford was glad to hear this as he had been nervous at the prospect of broadcasting live to the nation.

6B was a small drama production studio positioned in the central core of the building. It was built out of structural brick to reduce noise transmission between neighbouring studios. The studio shared a little triangular listening room with studio 6C linked by windows. Inside the listening room sat members of the production crew, all of them busy in front of banks of sound equipment and telephone sets.

Wilford was guided over to a ribbon microphone where he stood with his papers in his hand. He was told by Colin to wait for his cue. Colin pointed to a portly man in the listening room saying the man would give the signal for Wilford to commence his reading.

Wilford waited patiently and cleared his throat. As he sat, he watched Philip who was seated in the listening room, he was chatting in a relaxed manner with members of the production crew. Wilford wondered why on earth he had agreed to this instead of telling Phillip that he should find another reader to perform, probably one with more of this kind of experience and not prone to feeling pangs of nervous anxiety whenever they had to speak in public. He could already feel his mouth turning dry.

The first signal from the corpulent man came quickly, it spoke to Wilford telling him to get ready. He glanced down nervously at his papers. A recorded spoken introduction together with a baying mix of violins, piano, and clashing percussion played into the studio. Wilford wondered if the sombre tones of the speaker were those of Valentine Dyall himself. The melodramatic music diminished, and a second cue told him to begin his reading. He turned away from the microphone and cleared his throat, then he began to read from his papers. First, he introduced himself and spoke briefly about his writing career. He now proceeded to get on with his reading.

"The following story was told to me by a lady I interviewed whilst writing my second book, Old Haunts of Suburbia. To protect her identity, I will call her Glenda." Wilford's opening lines were slightly wobbly, but it was a good start and both Colin and Phillip gave him the thumbs up from the window looking into the listening room.

"Glenda was born and bred in the city of York. When Glenda was only eight years old her family suffered a terrible tragedy. Glenda's mother died from complications of influenza leaving behind her husband, Glenda's father, who we shall call Jack, and of course Glenda, and her baby brother Paul.

Being the only wage earner in the family, Jack had to leave both Glenda and her brother alone in the family home so that he could work out his night shifts in the bakery. The Bakery was two blocks away; almost one and a half miles. The following words are

Glenda's." Wilford gave a pause, sipped from a glass of water

(*wishing it was something stronger*) then continued.

"My father worked long and hard to provide for us when my mother passed away. We were only young, myself being only eight and my brother only four.

My father worked in a bakery all through the night and reluctantly had to leave us alone in the house during his shift. You see, we had no other family nearby.

My father would give us strict instructions that we should put ourselves to bed at nine o'clock, and no later. I took charge of helping my little brother Paul get ready for bed, and after we said our prayers, I would snuff out the candle.

We had a dog, a German shepherd called Benny that my father would leave outside tethered, with a lengthy chain, to the kennel to guard over us should any burglar try to ransack our house whilst my father worked through the night.

Every night that I assumed to be just past midnight, I would be woken by my father as he came back to check on us. I would pretend to be asleep with my eyes shut tight as his hand stroked over the covers slowly tucking me in. I knew he'd be cross if he was to find me still awake, but I always found it hard to sleep before midnight.

I always liked it when my father came to check on us every night, he would always leave the dog with us in my room. I could hear Benny's gentle panting as he lay down on the floor on our terrible threadbare carpet next to my bed. Sometimes I would reach down and touch his soft fur, and he would lick my fingertips as if to say, don't worry Glenda, I will guard you. And guard us he did, night after night, year after year.

One day my brother and I were eating breakfast, I was a little older then, maybe eleven, I'm not so sure. My Father came back from working his night shift at the bakery. I asked him why he always came home and checked on us, tucking me in and why he always left the dog to lie by my bed. I told him I was so grateful and that it always made me feel safe and secure.

You can imagine my surprise when he told me that he never once came back from work to tuck me in, and that the dog was never left with us in the bedroom but was always chained outside.

It was so dark in the bedroom without a light, I never looked down, not once to see what I thought was Benny lying on the floor. I wondered with horror what had been licking my fingertips, and what hot mouth and warm fur I had been stroking all these years. I wondered, and still do with some fear, who on earth had been tucking in the bedclothes all those dark, and lonely nights whilst my brother and I were alone in the house."

Wilford paused signifying that he'd finished his reading. He glanced over into the listening room. The portly man gave him a thumbs up and then turned to signal through the window into the adjoining studio 6C. After a short moment, the door to Wilford's studio was opened and Colin told him that he should come out and join the others in the listening room.

From the listening room, Wilford watched the play being performed from studio 6C. There was a group of people, two men and one woman. One of the men and the woman were reading off scripts whilst the second man produced sound effects using a variety of equipment. Currently, he was using a paper bag to create the effect of a burning fire.

Phillip congratulated Wilford on his recording, "Well done old boy, you managed to do it all in one go. Colin was impressed with your reading skills, he said it was good enough to rival Dyall himself." Phillip pointed to a large framed black & white photograph hanging on the wall in the listening room. It was a portrait of Valentine Dyall. Wilford studied the somewhat craggy features of the solemn looking man who stared out at him from the photograph, with slick hair as black as a raven's wing.

"Oh, I don't know about that. I think my talents lie solely on the printed page," replied Wilford.

"Well I think you might have a second career waiting in the wings old boy," Phillip said merrily as he gave him a light slap on the back.

When the play had finished, Colin told Wilford and Phillip that they had cut both sections together and it was about to be played out live. Wilford said that he wouldn't stay to listen as he considered the prospect of listening to himself rather cringeworthy.

During the live broadcast, Wilford had decided to go and find himself some refreshment in the form of a cup of tea. He wandered around the corridors and waiting areas on the sixth floor but was unable to find any beverage making appliances. Feeling despondent, he then came to a black, iron spiral staircase. The staircase stretched upwards not unlike the spine of some prehistoric reptile, connecting the sixth to the seventh floor, and its purpose was to allow actors to move quickly between studios.

He watched bewildered as water cascaded down the metal steps and pooled in the corridor below. Already the water was an inch or so in depth along the floor where he stood. He turned and decided to look for somebody to notify, guessing that there must be a burst water pipe upstairs.

He turned a dimly lit corridor and nearly bumped into a young, spectacled blond woman, who was carrying some papers, she almost dropped them in fright. Wilford apologised and explained about the water. She said that she should go and find Eric the caretaker, and then she promptly disappeared around the corner still clutching her documents.

Bored of waiting, and curious to see the plumbing disaster for himself he decided to peek upstairs. Once he'd climbed the staircase, he was standing in at least half a foot or more of dark murky water. The water was pouring with speed from underneath a set of double doors and was flowing down the staircase. He pushed open the double doors; it took some strength due to the force of the water pushing against them.

Stepping into a dimly lit corridor he stood dumbfounded when he saw the parallel rows of dim flickering lights running from each edge straight down the length of the passage. The very end of the corridor was gloomy; it was impossible for him to perceive anything beyond about twenty yards.

Shadows darkened the corners of the corridor, rounding them, giving the appearance of a tunnel. The marginal lights, what he could now see to be lanterns were undefined but clear enough to produce a weak gleam that created a rippling effect on the ceiling of the corridor like cold moonshine reflecting off deep water.

The walls of the corridor seemed to dissipate into a miasmic shroud created by shadows as they bled into one another blending and mixing. For a moment, he even thought that he could see a tessellation of rectangular crumbling brickwork.

As Wilford stood terrified because his mind could not accept what he was seeing, yet here it was presented to him in all it's frightening glory. It was the tunnel at Wormbridge. He could hear his heart thumping in his ears, feel the shortness of breath as his one lung tried hard to draw in the oxygen that his overburdening heart required. And then it happened.

The first faint whiff of smoke. A stomach churning, throat constricting stench of burning oil, mixed with something else, something disturbingly fatty. He tried with an unsteady hand to wipe away the scene before his eyes, but he only succeeded in producing a more defined spectacle as a shape appeared to bud from the dark shadows at the end of the tunnel.

The shape shuffled towards him, sloshing through the water. Wilford stood trembling, he felt his legs buckle as the shape took on a human aspect. Once it had scuffled close enough Wilford could see the true horror of it.

A badly burned and melted cadaverous form. The skin had peeled away in strips from its black charred body and hung limply down to the floor, trailing in the current of the water as it struggled to reach him. The hair on its head was singed to only a couple of centimetres from the scalp. Its hands were a melted pair of mitts composed of fused fingers, many burnt down to scorched bone. It was the creatures face, or lack of one, that provided the vision that Wilford knew in that instant to be something that he would carry with him always and even to the grave.

The head of the creature was a blackened globular mess of melted flesh; yet, a pair of bright eyeballs gleamed from charred sockets. It had no mouth but was struggling to speak out from sealed lips. He looked on in revulsion as crooked yellowed teeth began to chew a hole through where its mouth once sat. The creature spoke out to him through the gory fissure it had created, *'She keeps me here … she keeps me here … SHE KEEPS ME HERE!'* uttered the pitiful sight before him, but without a properly formed mouth, its utterances sounded more like *'See keets ne heer.'*

Wilford was now convinced that the once speculated inherited mental malaise was sadly real and was now causing him to experience another terminal fit of insanity. He began to hammer his forehead using both of his hands bunched into fists. He braced himself because he realised that in mere moments that odious figure would be upon him, it's blackened charbroiled face of death only inches from his own.

The corridor is suddenly flooded with light from four pendant domed ceiling lamps. The creeping charred figure had evaporated as though it was nothing more than some ephemeral vestige left over from a bad nightmare. The arched almost vaulted brickwork now replaced by stark plaster and textured ceiling tiles.

He looked down at the dry carpeted floor, the water had gone. He checked his shoes, and his trousers. They were completely dry. He then heard a gasp of shock from behind him. Turning, he saw a burley middle aged man, motionless, his finger resting on a bulging Bakelite lamp switch, his mouth open in astonishment.

In an instant, Wilford was able to read the expression that was stamped across the man's face, and he guessed rightly that he must be Eric, the caretaker. "You saw it didn't you?" spoke Wilford. For a moment Eric remained in his cataleptic state. Slowly his eyes moved from staring blankly down the brightly lit corridor and came to rest on Wilford's own wide eyes and fervent face.

"I-I-I don't ..."

"I know you saw it, you did, didn't you? Tell me you saw it!" snapped Wilford. Eric thought for a moment,

"Hey, what did you do? You did something, down there!" He pointed to the corridor, his hand still pressed against the light switch on the wall.

"What did you see? Did you see ... the thing?" pressed Wilford.

"I saw something, but-but you were doing it. Yes, that's right, it must've been you. Blimey, what are you?" Eric backed away and scuttled down the corridor and out of sight, obviously quite shaken. Wilford although quite unsettled himself let out a long, drawn sigh of relief. Checking his dry trousers for the umpteenth time he leaned against the corridor wall and began to laugh a nervous restrained laugh.

He had found Phillip shortly afterwards and told him that he was going to change the premise of his latest book from one of simply chronicling stories and encounters with ghosts, to one where he would attempt to obtain real evidence and present his findings within its pages. Phillip liked the sound of Wilford's idea, but he urged him to finish his current book on time. There was always room to change direction for any subsequent works if the latest book was to be as successful as its predecessor. Wilford assured him that his book would be finished on time before making his way back to his hotel.

***

Back in the Manvellian, Wilford was feverishly scratching down in his notebook everything he could remember about his experience at Broadcasting house. He suddenly felt as though he had a new lease of life. Gone were the fears that he was gradually succumbing to a degenerative mental condition. He could see it in the eyes of Eric the caretaker, the consummate horror across Eric's face spoke volumes and told Wilford he had not been a solitary observer of the ethereal scene played out before them both.

Seven

Wilford was now riding the first train back to Ulverstone. He had checked out of his hotel during the early hours of the morning. The previous evening, he had taken a taxi to *Jack's darkroom & camera store*, a shop specialising in photographic equipment on Oxford street. The cabbie recommended the shop and Wilford purchased a camera together with a few rolls of film.

The camera he bought was a Kodak Brownie Holiday Flash. It came with a non-synchronized flash unit for night use. He intended to use the camera to obtain as much tangible evidence as he could of the manifestations at the site of the old Wormbridge underpass.

Being new to photography he aimed to speak with his room neighbour, Preston when he finally got back to the Portside Inn. He hoped Preston would be able to give him a few pointers, and maybe even accompany him on his new mission.

Wilford hailed a taxi when he disembarked from the train at Ulverstone, coincidentally, it was the same driver who had originally driven him to the station on the night he'd left for London, he recognised him straight away.

The cabbie made small talk telling him how the weather had taken a turn for the worse, and he had to agree when he saw the sleet showering down and turning the roads and the gravel path leading up to the Inn into a slushy potage.

Unpacked and refreshed from his journey, Wilford rapped on Preston's door, but he received no answer. He scrawled a fast note explaining his intentions and asking him for any help he could offer in the way of camerawork expertise. He explained that once he'd collected his boat from the Bell boatyard following servicing he would be moored near to the spot where 'you *had kindly donated your handkerchief.*' He slid the note under Preston's door before making his way downstairs.

Burt greeted Wilford as they passed on the stairs, "I saw you were back, I just wanted to give you this," he handed Wilford a letter, "vicar dropped it off himself he did." Wilford glanced at the envelope and then folded the letter and slid it into his inside coat pocket.

"Thank you, it will be the information I needed for my book, from the churchyard. I don't suppose you've seen Mr Haistwell this morning, only he wasn't in his room."

"Yes, I did sir. He went out this morning, early. Not sure when he'll be back."

"It doesn't matter, I left him a note. He'll know where to find me." Wilford said goodbye to Burt before leaving the Inn.

The cabbie was right about the weather. The climate had declined considerably since he had last sailed the cut. Wearing his warmest coat, hat and gloves, and with a thick woollen scarf tied up close to his chin, he still felt the air chilling him to the marrow as he steered *Knotty Buoy* on a course for the Bell Boatyard.

Although the flat, fat snowflakes melted the instant they touched the water, they were sticking to the cold decking on the boat forming a slippery surface on which to walk. He was mindful of the fact that he would shortly have locks to operate and knew that he'd have to be extra careful when manoeuvring around the boat.

As the course widened, he knew that he was within the vicinity of Wormbridge. He waited for the bank to come into view and he saw the prickly bush growing in front of where the tunnel mouth once supported the brickwork structure.

Preston's handkerchief was just about visible in the temporarily blinding blizzard; he could still see it knotted to the bush, an iced rigid memento of his and Preston's previous visit together. He sailed onward.

Preston entered the bar of the Inn and he made a brief attempt to search for any sign of Wilford. He'd found the note pushed under his door the moment he'd returned from a brisk morning walk with his camera; he had wanted to capture images of the winter sunrise along with the snowy banks lining the canals.

Without any sign of Wilford in the room he made a line for the bar where he found Burt and his wife Joan. Preston greeted the pair and asked after Joan's health, she told him she was feeling much better and asked him if he was needing any breakfast, "No, thank you. I was looking for another guest, Mr Bailey, Wilford Bailey. He left me a note, he was asking for my help but I'm afraid I missed him."

Joan left the bar and went through to the kitchen behind. Burt placed the tankard he was drying back on a shelf next to the large brass bell and cord. He leaned on the bar and beckoned Preston to come closer as though what he had to say next was for his ears alone. "Some friendly advice sir. If I were you,

I'd stay clear away from Mr Bailey. Oh, don't get me wrong, he's a nice enough chap, no doubt about that. It's just I think he's a bit troubled sir, up 'ere," Burt placed a finger to his own temple.

"I'm sorry, what on earth do you mean?" asked Preston confused with what Burt was suggesting.

"Well ... I've noticed things, is all I'm saying sir," Preston was puzzled.

"I'm not sure I'm following you, could you be more specific?" Before Burt could answer he was called into the kitchen by Joan, but before he went, he added, "I'm only telling you this because you've been a patron at the Portside for many years, and a respected guest if I say so myself. I just think you should be careful is all. Now I'm sorry sir but my good lady wife needs me for some thing or other. But be mindful of what I said sir." Preston thanked Burt for his remarks,

"Actually, I will have that breakfast if I may," he said.

As Wilford cruised around the bend in the cut, he noticed a figure walking along the tow path. As he came closer, he was surprised to see that it was Corinne. She was carrying a basket and wearing a hooded red coat. The snow had settled on the hood and shoulders of her coat, yet she didn't seem to mind the chilly weather and walked with a sprightly gait.

Wilford steered the boat closer to the bank. As he approached, he called out to her. At first, she didn't hear him and ambled on, but eventually she turned and shielded her eyes with her gloved hand. Wilford gave her a broad wave, she smiled when she recognised him. He brought *Knotty Buoy* carefully to the edge of the towpath until the fenders bumped against the snow-covered cobbles.

Carefully, he jumped down onto the towpath and invited Corinne to come on-board, "Oh I'm not sure, how far are you going?"

"Only to the boatyard, then I intend to take a stroll into town, maybe get some lunch. We could lunch together if you like," he said hopefully. Corinne cast her eyes over the slippery looking deck,

"You'll have to help me, or I fear I may get a soaking," she said. Wilford held her gloved hand strongly and gave her support to climb on board.

"There's a nice fire in the stove below, you can warm yourself up while I get him out to the middle again," he said whilst taking up a position at the tiller.

"I'm not in the least bit cold. I love this weather, don't you? It's so ... invigorating!" Wilford smiled as she took up a position alongside him at the stern.

166

***

As they approached the locks on the course towards the boatyard, Wilford became aware of a wailing sound. He could just make out the form of a woman as she was bent half over the lock beams. She seemed to be in distress.

Wilford asked Corinne to keep the boat steady as he put the engine in neutral. She dutifully took hold of the tiller as the pair of them wondered what all the commotion was about.

Jumping down onto the icy path, Wilford ran over to the woman, an elderly woman. She was blubbering and shouting desolately into the lock behind the gates. "What is it, what on earth has happened?" he asked. She pointed down into the watery abyss below, the roar of the flooding water drowning both their voices.

"My Manfred, he's drowning down there, oh please, god please help him!" she cried. Wilford saw a narrowboat that appeared to be jammed and filling up with water. "He can't swim!" she continued to cry whilst holding her head. Wilford could just make out the form of a white-haired man, he was clinging to the top of a wheel house and shouting in blind panic as great torrents of water surged down from the lock gates, almost knocking him off the boat. "I got off to help with the lock, but I must've got it wrong, oh god help him!" Wilford saw the name of the boat painted in a lavish script along the side, just visible above the waterline, *Edna's Angel*. He recognised the name instantly as the boat that had passed him out on the water the night his engine died.

Wilford could see that the tiller was jammed into part of the lock holding the boat down. *Edna's Angel* was almost covered as Wilford ran back to his own boat and collected up a spare length of mooring rope. Corinne came to help him, "Wilford what's happened?"

"There's a man trapped in the lock, he's going to drown unless I can get him out of there!"

"Oh, how awful. Can I help?"

"Help me carry the rope, see it stays untangled," he said as he ran as fast as he could on the slick path.

When he reached the lock, Wilford tied a loop in the end of the mooring rope and then he threw it down into the rapidly filling lock. "Here, take hold of this!" he roared and watched as the old man below tried to grab the rope. "When you get it, hold on and put your foot in the loop." He watched as the old man who had understood him tried several times to grab the rope, but his hands were numb from the icy water. Eventually, he managed it and he stuck his boot in the loop.

"Please help him, I don't want him to die, please," the old woman cried. Wilford ignored her in his haste to free Manfred. He wound his end of the rope around a stout mooring bollard and used it for leverage to help pull Manfred up.

As he pulled on the rope, he could hear boots crunching through shingle and ice as the lockkeeper appeared. He took in the scene and raced over to Wilford to help haul Manfred the final few feet and onto the bank.

Wilford gasped for air and the old woman flung herself on top of her bedraggled husband, "Oh Manfred you stupid, stupid lubber, I thought I'd lost you," she cried onto his chest. Manfred sat up and spat a mouthwash of dirty water,

"Thank you, thank you," he said to Wilford who was still too tired to answer; he simply nodded to acknowledge the gratitude. Corinne came over to help Wilford to his feet. The lockkeeper glanced into the lock,

"Need a winch or crane to lift that out,' he said. "How'd you mange that?" he asked the elderly pair who were now slowly getting to their feet, Manfred was wet through and shivering. Wilford removed the contents of his coat pockets then took off his coat and placed it around Manfred's shoulders he thanked

Wilford again before stopping and staring over at the lock gates.

"It was the water, somehow the incoming water pushed me boat back, and it got jammed. But it wasn't just that. It was her I tell you, I seen her. When you pulled me up, she was looking over the lock beams, looking at me! Oh Edna, I want to go home." Wilford wanted Manfred to elaborate further on what he'd said.

"When you said you saw her, who did you mean?" Manfred's eyes were wild and staring, looking around him as he spoke,

"I saw Aggie, she was the one who did it, she wanted me dead, like she wants us all dead. I saw her face, white as snow and sneering at me from atop the gates." The old woman turned to Wilford,

"Thank you young man you saved my Manfred, you saved him. If it wasn't for you he'd be ..." she broke off and continued to sob as the lockkeeper told them both to go inside his cottage to warm up and dry off. He then turned to Wilford,

"You saved a man's life today, well done lad," he said.

"You helped me to pull him up, if you hadn't I don't think-"

"No, the credit's all yours, I won't hear of it. Now you want to come inside and warm up sir?" Wilford thanked the keeper but declined the offer.

"We best get back, there's no going forward to the boatyard now," Wilford said pointing at the lock.

"Aye right you are about that, that lot will take some shifting, and in this weather too!" The lockkeeper followed the two elderly boaters as they made a path for the limewashed cottage. Wilford and Corinne climbed back aboard *Knotty Buoy*. Soon they had reversed the boat and turned to face the way they'd come.

On the way back, they moored the boat near Ulverstone town. Unable to find a suitable place to eat that was open for business, they opted instead for some fish and chips. Missing his coat, Wilford shivered, and he held his bundle of food close to his chest as they hurriedly made a line down the treacherous snowy bank. Soon they were both back inside *Knotty Buoy* and warming themselves by the stove.

Wilford ate his fish and chips heartily whilst Corinne only picked at hers. The stove had been well fuelled and with the vents closed down, the coal within burned slower and hotter. He showed her his new camera as they sat at the single wooden table, "I intend to use this to try to capture evidence of Aggie, who haunts these waterways." He didn't try to hide his thoughts anymore. "I know it's all true. You see, I've seen things. Not Aggie exactly, but things nevertheless." She looked at him forlornly.

"Are you sure you weren't mistaken?"

"No Corinne, I wasn't. The last time I even had a witness, although he was too afraid to be of any real use at the time." Wilford cleared away the remnants of their meal, Corinne handed him her almost untouched package which he disposed of into a dustbin near the stove.

"And you are going to use this to do it?" she said as she held his camera, turning it over in her hands.

"That's the idea. Surely, if I can see something with my own eyes I can take a picture of it, no?"

"I wouldn't know Wilford, I don't know why proof is so important. Surely the stories themselves, and the belief that the locals have is enough?"

"Stories without evidence are just stories Corinne, like Robin Hood, or King Arthur of Camelot. What I aim to do is take one such story and lift it out of the mists of myth and show it to the people for what it actually is."

"And what is that?"

"A real, living, breathing legend. A spirit of a tragic woman who still walks among us. Don't you see, it would be proof that there is life after death, that there is something else other than what we think we know. It might deter us from starting wars if we know we might walk the earth for eternity, trapped as an earthbound soul because of the wrongs we have done. It might make us all better people." Corinne, still looking somewhat glum and in contrast to Wilford's own animated face said,

"Some people say that we are not ready to know the mysteries of life. They say that man is responsible for his problems because he creates them."

"Who says that?"

"Well, my mother for one. She also says that we must accept that too much of who we are will never be truly understood."

"Forgive me Corinne, your mother sounds like a clever woman, but I disagree. I believe we are all on the boundary of understanding who we are. I want to help us get there." He took hold of Corinne's cool hands and looked deeply into her blue eyes that seemed almost endless. "I would very much like you to help me."

Preston was sorting through the latest batch of developed photographs he had recently collected from the pharmacy in town. He made two piles of pictures, those that he considered worth keeping and those he would discard. As he worked, his mind wandered over what Burt had told him after breakfast.

He'd waited for Burt to come over to his table to collect away his breakfast things and he had asked him again to explain why he had tried to warn him off regarding Wilford. Burt had sat down at his table. He told him that he and others had witnessed Wilford talking to himself as though having a real conversation with somebody else, only there was nobody else with him. He also told Preston that on occasion he would order two drinks and leave one opposite an empty chair as though he had a companion.

Preston couldn't fathom this at all. Wilford to him had seemed a well-balanced, stable, sensible sort of fellow. He did have a thing for ghosts, but Preston understood that it was how he made his living. If everyone was persecuted for adopting unconventional interests, then he himself would be put under scrutiny for spending so much of his time huddled in small shelters, whilst waiting for a chance to capture the image of a kingfisher or even a lesser redpoll.

He stopped sorting his pictures and again read the note that Wilford had left for him. He noticed how the writing appeared to have been applied to the paper with haste. Was this the writing of a man excited by discovery or a man worried and in need of help?

From what Burt had said he began to wonder if Wilford was indeed suffering from an affliction of some kind, after all, he had presented Preston with a conundrum regarding a missing junction that neither of them could find an explanation for. He did seem genuinely convinced by what he had seen and where he had seen it, and this obviously worried him thought Preston. He sighed heavily because he wasn't sure what he should do next.

***

It was about three in the afternoon. The snow had stopped falling, but the shrill winds were whipping up a resilient breeze. The sky had taken on even more sombre tones. With the white snow lining the banks, and the dark colour of the water, the whole scene resembled one of Preston's monochromatic snaps.

Wilford had used a thick woollen blanket to wrap around himself as he stood on the deck steering the vessel on which he and Corinne stood. The air had become frozen, jellified. It hurt him to breathe as though spiders had woven a thick cobweb lining within his lung.

A premature slit of rose pink, mixed with orange light peeked between the heavy grey cloud cover and shone with enough intensity and power to keep up the entire heavens singlehanded, long enough to hold off the inevitable decline into night.

And, from not so very far away shone another light, an unnatural yet inviting light.

Knotty Buoy had cruised into the swollen area of the river course from where the old Wormbridge junction once joined. He pointed out the dancing lights to Corinne, "You see them, you see the lanterns?" Corinne nodded.

"I do Wilford, I see them."

"And the tunnel, you see the tunnel?"

"I do see it." Wilford stood tall and shrugged off his blanket, *then I'm not going mad*, he thought to himself as the engine on the boat coughed out of life.

Knotty Buoy now only moved under the influence of the wind as it gently pushed him towards the lantern lined tunnel ingress.

Gone was the large thorny bush where Preston had left his motif, gone was the high bank of long windswept sod and scattered brick. Instead, was a huge dark imbibing maw. As the boat passed into the tunnel, Wilford felt as though he had reached a point where he was powerless to retreat. As he felt the first drops of cold impure water hit his head from the underside of the roof of the tunnel, he thought that perhaps at this point he had strayed too far from home.

The boat jolted to a stop. Corinne and Wilford almost toppled from the stern. "The boat's hit something I think," said Corinne.

"No, it's her, it's Aggie." Wilford said anxiously and guided Corinne below deck. She sat on a bunk waiting to hear what he intended to do next." He picked up his camera and attempted to adjust the flash unit, but it was so dark inside the boat, in the tunnel, that he simply placed the camera strap around his neck. The flames in the stove provided their only source of illumination.

He flicked a switch for the electric wall lights, but he knew in his heart that all electric lighting, including the horn and the headlamp up top wouldn't work.

"I'll have to light the oil lamps," he said indicating the wall mounted lamps between the portholes. He searched for matches but couldn't find any, he delved in his trouser pockets and pulled out the letter the vicar had left for him at the Inn. He took out a single folded piece of paper from the envelope and left it face up on the table, then he twisted the envelope into a paper horn and poked it into the flames within the stove.

With the envelope now burning, he used it to light the wicks of both oil lamps and adjusted them providing enough light so that they could both see. He came over to Corinne and took her hand in his, "Don't worry, I will look after you, it's only a tunnel. If we must, we can walk out on the towpath." Corinne watched as he began to adjust his camera.

"What are you expecting to see?" she asked.

"Aggie, a burned boat, I don't know, but whatever is out there this time I'm ready." He was about to tell her that she should wait for him below deck while he went back up top, but his eyes caught sight of the note he'd removed from the envelope.

The reverend Mathew Fell, true to his word had copied out the record from the parish register, the record recounting the original inscription on the broken gravestone in the cemetery. In a rather bold hand and probably using a dip nib pen and Indian ink, the reverend had penned:

IN MEMORY OF
MAGGIE DARCEL
BELOVED DAUGHTER, MOTHER AND WIFE.
CORINNE DARCEL (COCO)
DAUGHTER OF MAGGIE DARCEL
REUNITED IN THE ARMS OF THE LORD

Wilford could hear the silence between his heartbeats as he read again the inscription. He lifted his gaze to rest on Corinne's face. She was now standing away from the table, under her arm, in the thick woollen folds of her red coat nestled a bemired doll. Her lips were pursed together in guilt as she looked at him. "You. You're the child, the girl. It's you ... Coco. It's a pet name, something your mother ..." he broke off in silence to stare at her. Corinne continued to stand in muteness, but eventually the corners of her mouth curled upwards to display a happy but almost regretful smile.

"I'm sorry Wilford, I should have told you. But I thought you were nice, and I wanted ... I wa-" Three loud raps filled the boat and it rocked slightly with each pound. The flames on the oil lamps lowered almost to obscurity. The raps came again.

Wilford fell onto a cushioned bunk. He fingered the note containing the inscription, not wanting to believe what had to be believed. "It's my mother, I should go to her. Thank you Wilford, for bringing me here. I have been hearing her, sensing her, but never knowing how to find her. I couldn't see the lights you see, not on my own." The sound of Corinne's voice was changing and becoming higher in pitch; losing the womanly tones, becoming childlike.

Now Wilford could only see a child standing before him, a mere girl with only the budding features to show the woman she would have grown to be. The child of Coco stood in an oversized coat, clutching a doll as though it was an extra vital limb. "But you're just a child, where, how...?"

"All children are adult spirits, we are born in a newly grown body, when I died, I went back into the world of spirits," she said dryly.

"What is it you want?"

"To be reunited with my mother. To help her find her way."

"And me, what happens to me?" A further series of three raps shook the boat. Wilford had to grip the table to prevent himself rolling from his seat. When he looked up, Coco was gone.

Standing back on the deck Wilford peered into the dimness of the tunnel. It would have been much darker if not for the parallel rows of oddly radiant lanterns, each a duplicate of the one before it. From where he stood on the bow, he could see the last few minutes of daylight filtering inside the far exit of the tunnel, the warm orange sunbeams sparkling lazily from the water's surface.

On the towpath near the exit he saw a diminutive figure stood perched on the edge of the bank, expectant. It was Coco. He then saw something else. Within the scintillating ring of vermillion sunlight, he saw a figure rise from the water.

Although it was quite a distance away, he could still make out the head and shoulders as it remained fixed in the cold swirling currents. He saw Coco slide into the water and swim over to the static almost graceless mass of weed and carcass. For a moment, both water-borne beings embraced each other.

Wilford raised his camera and began to take pictures of the tunnel, the lanterns, and the figures in the water. His camera flash malfunctioned almost every time he operated the shutter. In frustration he cast aside the camera and cupped his mouth with his hands, then shouted down the tunnel, "End it now Aggie, leave these people in peace. Find peace for yourself, for Coco. For pity's sake end it."

His words rebounded, echoing from the brickwork and rang in his ears for some time after he'd finished. He could no longer see the figures in the water, the curtain of night had finally been drawn. He watched mesmerised as one by one the lanterns blinked into extinction. *'Cut your lights out ...'* When the final lantern vanished, he was plunged into solid darkness.

Alone in the dark he used his hands to feel his way around the deck, he intended to try switching on the engine so that he could reverse out of the tunnel. He became aware of the rhythmic sound of horses trotting, the sound was coming from somewhere above him, over him. The clip, clop from the iron shoes rang out, penetrating through the brickwork above, the brickwork that shouldn't exist but roofed him all the same.

Suddenly the clip, clops became less rhythmic, more erratic. The cries and yells of men now became audible to Wilford, and there was panic in those strange and somehow hollow voices. Snorts and whinnying began to issue from somewhere above, the cries of men now audible, '*Git the nags goin' they're standin' tight, the cart's tippin'.*'

A tumultuous cracking and creaking rang out. The sound of phantom men and horses shrieking in fear as they plunged into the waters below. The pummelling of free-falling bricks hitting the water, smashing into man and beast and boat. Wilford's body was delivered yet another hammering blow as bricks, that shouldn't exist, rained down pulverising the decking on *Knotty Buoy*, breaking holes in the hull.

The boat on which Wilford now lay bleeding groaned like an old animal caught by a whaler's harpoon as its gore spilled into the water, mixing with the oil and the silt. Only it wasn't *Knotty Buoy's* blood, it was Wilford's. And as he sank down into the merciless bitter water, amongst splintered plank, twisted metal and shattered glass, he realised in his last living moments that he would forever lay entombed under that raised secluded bank with nothing more than a barbed scrub as a grave marker.

Eight

reston Haistwell peered unseen through the narrow gap of his open doorway. He watched as Burt unlocked the adjacent door, Wilford's room. Burt was followed into the room by three men, two were uniformed police officers, the third, Preston assumed to be a detective.

All four men spent quite some time rummaging around in Wilford's things. Preston wished that he could hear what they were saying because the disappearance of his room neighbour had been the talk of the Inn, and no doubt also the town.

There had been no sight or sound of Wilford since he'd left the Inn that fateful night. Preston still had the note that Wilford had left for him. He had studied the note many times and now feared that something terrible had happened to him. He felt guilt ridden that he had not responded to his request for help.

According to Burt, Howard Durnsten the proprietor of the Rose and Castle boat hire was convinced that Wilford had simply taken off, boat and all. The police had already dredged stretches of the canals fearing an accident but have since found nothing.

It was Phillip Letts, Wilford's publisher who had been certain that there may be some nefarious reason behind his associate's disappearance. he had explained to the police how out of character it was for him to simply disappear and remain incommunicado.

Burt had told Preston that during his many interviews with the police, he had kept him out of *'this messy business'*, telling him that there was no reason for him to get involved. It might cause him some *'mischief'* if the police were to know that they had both been acquainted. Preston insisted that he was happy to help the police with their enquiries but admitted that he wouldn't really be of much help other than offering them the note that had been left for him.

Preston watched as the four men left Wilford's room. The suited man, the detective, was carrying a dark maroon case. *Princess 300 portable typewriter* was written in metallic script along the side of the case. He watched as Burt locked the room before speaking to the police men, "Do you have any idea when I can clear out the room for patron use?" The detective spoke,

"Not yet sir, not until we've closed our enquiries. This room is still an active crime scene. But it shouldn't take much longer before we find him, we've a couple of boats gone up Macclesfield way and another on the way to Llangollen." Preston almost walked out his room to give the policeman the note which he was clutching in his clammy hand, but Burt had spotted him, lurking behind his door. He gave Preston a wink and a look to tell him that it'd be best if he stayed put, for now at least.

***

Another two weeks had passed, Preston was almost at the end of his current stay at the Portside Inn. It would soon be Christmas, and the Inn would close for business. He had accepted an invitation to stay with his brother down in Devon for the duration of the festive period.

The heavy snowfalls of late had all but melted away leaving behind traces that lingered in the corners of carparks or at the trailing ends of old towpaths where the snow had been collected by shovel and compacted.

Even though Christmas was only around the corner, the climate had turned surprisingly milder. There was even the hint of the slim green blades of daffodils as they tentatively emerged from the sheltered slopes of many a canal bank.

Preston had been sat eating his picnic lunch on one such river bank. He had only finished consuming his ham and pickle sandwich that the Portside had provided for him that morning when he saw the sheen of deep teal as it darted in a line from one side of the bank to another. He almost choked on the bolus of ham and bread in his surprise and subsequent haste reaching for the binoculars that hung from a strap around his neck.

With the binoculars fixed to his own eyes he marvelled at the sight of the Kingfisher, as it continued to dart and dive into the water, its short, rounded wings whirring until they became a mere blur. Suddenly the waterside jewel was gone. Preston stood and perused the banks for another sighting of the bird he had been looking for all the many weeks during his recent stay near Ulverstone.

He came down the side of the bank heavily, almost slipping on the long damp tufty grass. As he now stood on the towpath, he saw something floating on the surface of the water. He saw that it was a piece of wood, a splintered broken shard of timber and it was inscribed.

Preston snapped a long thin branch from a bare willow tree close by and he used this to poke at the floating wood, teasing it towards him. When it was almost touching the edge of the bank he reached down and fished it out. Turning the dripping varnished plank over in his hands he read the inscription, '*Knotty Bu-*' it read, the rest of the wording sheared off and now lost somewhere out on the river, or beneath.

The sopping words he held in his hands instantly hit a spot in his memory, conjuring up a day on the water. As he looked around, he hadn't realised until now that he had somehow, perhaps instinctively ambled along the same banks where he and Wilford had sailed that day hoping to find the answer to the mysterious, unidentified junction that had worried Wilford so much.

He now became aware of something flapping in the wind across the water. There was something caught on that large prickly bush where he had once tied a handkerchief. A rag or cloth, whatever it was it was pinned by the thorns trapping it like an abandoned military tunic on barbed wire.

Lifting the binoculars to his face he inspected the scene more closely. The cloth was large and white, and an ashen almost featureless face appeared to hang above it like it was swathed in some ghastly death shroud.

The manifestation gave Preston a fright. He dropped the wooden plank to slap the water's surface. Droplets of cold mire were sent upwards to splatter his face. Wiping his face dry with the sleeve of his woollen jacket he searched the far bank, only a bare spiny bush stood beating in the wind.

Unable to believe he had imagined the thing he'd seen, he looked down, searching for the fragment of *Knotty Buoy*, he saw it drifting outwards, the weak sunlight reflected from the shiny, wet, veneered surface. Then all at once, the drifting wood seemed to be sucked down. Pulled into the deep, dark water almost by hand as though it was only ever released as a hint, a warning to others like him that there are hidden depths to all questions.

Perturbed by the things he'd witnessed, he returned towards the Inn with haste in his steps.

The End

***

The author would appreciate an Amazon and Goodreads review.

I do read all the reviews each and every one and I am very grateful to anyone who has taken the time to post a review. I appreciate the time you have taken reading this book. I hope you enjoyed reading it as much as I enjoyed writing it.

You are welcome to join David on his Facebook page and group where you can receive news about forthcoming releases, and also to discuss and share thoughts and queries about any of David's published works.

https://www.facebook.com/davidralphwilliams

For more information on the complete range of David Ralph Williams' fiction visit David's website:

https://davidralphwilliams.webs.com

More Ghost Stories by David Ralph Williams:

Olde Tudor – A ghost story

When Alistair Swift, a retired school teacher buys an old Tudor cottage in the ancient town of Thornbarrow, he soon discovers that his rural retreat is anything but the peaceful getaway he had hoped for. In fact, he becomes the owner of two homes. One, a delightful Tudor cottage. The other, an ancient sepulchral cavern. The land on which they both stand a once sacred site in prehistory. Alistair's practiced curiosity finds him meddling with things that should remain untouched. Cut off from the rest of the town by bad weather and sick with fever, he is tormented by something beyond the tangible world.

Olde Tudor – A ghost story (extract)

The next morning Alistair woke feeling worse with his illness. The headaches were more intense. His nose was blocked, and his sinuses were heavily congested exacerbating his headaches. The random cycles of sweats then chills were uncomfortable enough, and his muscles ached. Wrapping a woollen bedsheet around himself, and sliding his feet into a pair of slippers, he slowly made his way down to the kitchen.

He intended to make himself a pot of tea as his throat was still painful and very dry, and because the house was freezing cold. Ice clung to the inside of every window. The coldness from the stone flagged floor was already beginning to penetrate upwards through his slippers.

He clumsily cleaned out the wood stove and added fresh kindling, then he looked for his box of matches. After a fruitless search he remembered that he had dropped them in the cave during the previous day's exploration. Realising he was unable to light the stove, or in fact anything in the house, he slammed down his tea caddy in frustration.

Parting the kitchen curtains, he peered outside through the iced leaded window panes. The snow was deep. Almost a couple of feet in places. The wind had caused drifting. He opened the back door and a pile of snow toppled inwards covering his feet. Shaking the snow off his slippers he closed the door. Smokey entered the kitchen, his meows and purring signified that he was hungry again.

Feeling disheartened after imagining what a nice treat a pot of hot tea and a fried kipper would have been, Alistair went over to the small pantry to collect a bottle of milk. He poured some into a saucer on the kitchen floor. Smokey lapped it up greedily.

Still wrapped in his bedclothes Alistair searched high and low for a second box of matches. He poked about in the dead fire grates for a trace of a glowing cinder. He thought if he found one he might be able to use it to coax the woodstove into life. There was none. What was he supposed to do now he pondered? Rub sticks together like a caveman?

He tried his phone line again, but it was still dead, as were the lights and other electrics in the house. The wind had picked up again, it was whipping around the house cooling it down even further. He thought that the best course of action was to go back to his bed and keep as warm as possible. He was feeling terrible. He desperately hoped that his power and communication lines would soon be remedied, but the weather outside probably meant more delays.

He weakly carried a ceramic jug over to the sink; intending to fill it with water so that he could place it by his bedside. Always best to keep your fluids up, he remembered his doctor once telling him. He turned the tap, but nothing came out. The pipes must be frozen solid he guessed. Returning to the pantry, he took the only remaining milk and some sliced ham. He went back to his bed. After eating a couple of slices of ham, he settled back into his bed and fell into a spate of broken sleep.

He woke with a hacking cough. Each cough made his head throb. The light was failing in the bedroom. He picked up his wristwatch from the bedside cabinet and could barely make out that it read a half past three. He had slept most of the day. Taking hold of the half bottle of milk he took small sips, small enough that his aching throat would allow. He used his only remaining handkerchief to clear his nose.

Glancing at the dead fire grate he realised that he must go back into the cave to find the matches. His illness was steadily getting worse and he feared that he would catch his death if he didn't get himself warm. He would have to do it whilst he still had the strength. But not tonight. The weather was frightful, and the night had almost fallen. He would try in the morning. As he thought about this course of action, he became aware of a sound.

Lying with the bedclothes pulled tightly around his head, partly to keep himself warm, but mostly to obscure the ghastly sounds that had begun to fill his bedroom, Alistair lay paralysed with fear. The breathing had started suddenly. The same bestial snorts and pants that had frightened him whilst he was in the cave. They sounded as though they were just outside of his bedroom window.

The ancient ash, all old and gnarled was the only thing that could provide height for any creature outside that wanted to taunt him. And taunt him it did. He didn't dare look across to the window.

With only the ghost of the day's light lingering he feared that if he did look, he might see it. The thing that his subconscious mind had concocted back in the cave. The thing that he had been trying so desperately hard to push back further and further into the dark crepuscular recesses of his mind but was failing with every new second to do so. "Away!" he croaked hoarsely. "For pity's sake, leave me be!"

With his final words the breathing stopped. His heart now in his mouth, he lowered the bedsheet just enough for him to take a gulp of cool air. If he had light in his room, he would have seen his exhaled breath hang before him, a frozen nebulous cloud of vapour, slowly dissipating away like a phantom searching for a dark place in which to hide itself.

As he sat up in bed still breathing hard, palpitations thumping against his festering chest cavity, a new sound rang out. The sound was outside. Some distance from the house. He knew exactly the source and cause of the sound. It was the gate to the cavern slamming shut.

Dead Men's Eyes – A ghost story

When Frankie looked down at the dead clown in the coffin with its whitened features and lifeless eyes now closed with copper lids, he never thought that stealing money from the dead would have such serious consequences for years to come.

There was something cold, something unsettling about the Happy Fair penny arcade, and now it was hers. Tamela could feel it, as though the place was alive, watching her and listening to her as she opened its doors for the first time in twenty years. Pieces of the past had lingered, enclosed within like old crisp leaves from a forgotten summer.

Perhaps it was the white mask of the original owner, Jolly Roger, an old-time circus clown whose likeness was still branded onto the very walls of the Happy Fair to remind those within who is the one and true owner. Soon whoever is foolish enough to pass through its doors begins to learn that lives can shatter just like old bones can crumble, and Tamela's fear grows when she thinks that she may have lost the most important and most precious thing in her life.

Dead Men's Eyes – A ghost story (extract)

Frankie Singer stood in the doorway to the parlour and stared at the casket, he was alone with the body. He then entered the room and tiptoed towards the coffin. He kept a lookout for his father because he wasn't supposed to be in the repose room. He should only be here when he had his chores to do, and when there was something new to learn, but only when his father was present.

Sidney Erebus had been embalmed by his father and was laid to rest as his wishes dictated, in full make up and attire of his alter ego Jolly Roger, the eminent ex sideshow clown. Frankie edged towards the coffin, he lifted the lid and peered inside. The colours hit him all at once and the garish mix was enough to raise his gorge. He fought a reflex to wretch, swallowing it back down.

Sidney, or Roger, was laid flat, his arms rigid by the sides of his Auguste all-in-one chequered suit. He wore ruffles at the neck and cuffs, and his bright red wig had been carefully fixed to his scalp using a fine thread, the same thread used to sew his eyes and mouth shut. He had a Ping-Pong ball painted red fitted over the end of his nose. His mouth was a glossy smile that almost met both earlobes. Resting on Roger's eyes was a pair of copper pennies, which had been polished, so they shone like new.

Frankie was only thirteen years old, but he already knew a lot of the trade secrets used in the funeral and embalming business. It was Frankie's father's intention that he would work in the family business, eventually taking over from him as did his father from Frankie's grandfather. Frankie wasn't all that thrilled with the idea, preferring an alternative career. His obsession with making things from metal model construction kits gave him aspirations of being a mechanic or an engineer. He also dreamed of a career in the navy as he wanted to see other places, far off places away from his father's dusty, musty funeral parlour.

Frankie studied the copper coins resting on Roger's eyes. He'd seen his father the previous day, boiling the pennies in a small saucepan in a salt-vinegar mixture to remove the patina. It was something his father always did as a tradition when dressing the body. Once, Frankie had asked him why he placed the pennies on the eyes. 'To pay the ferryman,' his father told him, 'so the dead can be taken across the Styx to the underworld where they can rest in peace.' He had learned from his father, that the Styx was a mythological river that formed a boundary between earth and the afterlife.

Frankie stared at Roger. He noticed how his father had applied the white grease paint carefully but had still managed to smear a lot of it on the red wig, at the point where it rested on Roger's forehead. Roger himself would never have been so careless; his make-up was always meticulously applied and although Frankie's father had something of the artistic streak in him, (a quality that helped his career in embalming greatly), he wasn't able to reproduce the make-up with the same faultlessness as the wearer used to manage from forty years of applying it to his own face.

Roger had been a famous clown at a travelling circus, where he'd performed slapstick as well as many incredulous balancing acts within the accompanying sideshow, or freakshow as some indecorous people referred to it. For some reason he left the circus, some said under a dark cloud, and the rumour mill started.

They said, Sidney Erebus had something of an 'oddity' about him. He suffered from an unusual bone disorder where, according to those ex co-workers at the circus, he could spend many weeks crippled with his legs and arms in plaster saying that his bones had 'crumbled', and then later making a remarkable and full recovery. He claimed that he was able to treat himself by indulging in a 'much-needed dose of revitalisation', as he explained it.

A doctor who once treated him, had broken patient confidentiality and written an article in a medical journal which was picked up in the Times, where he mentioned the disease that Sidney suffered from to be something of a 'medical anomaly'. The doctor explained that he would suffer episodes of complete breakdown of his bones, only to have them inexplicably regenerated in a miraculous and yet unknown feat of biological chemistry.

There were many who said Sidney worked on the sideshow because that was where he belonged, with all the other irregularities of nature. Sidney reputedly had a particularly disturbing mannerism. It had long been known that he had a habit of harming children. Many refused to believe such an affront to his character, as he had been involved in many philanthropic acts helping the less fortunate, (especially children in need) spanning the whole of the country, but there were the stories. Stories from children, and from parents of children whom he had harmed, and Frankie knew one such child, his best friend Bill Coveley.

All the children loved Jolly Roger, as is the old adage, 'all the world loves a clown,' and they travelled in droves to see him perform. He would have them all laughing in hysterics at his amusing antics. Sometimes, not too often, but nevertheless frequently enough, Roger would appear away from the performance ring, out of sight from the watchful eyes of the ringmaster.

If you were one of those children who didn't listen to your parents, (like Bill Coveley) who sometimes wandered off when they shouldn't have, (like Bill Coveley) who would poke about nosily finding themselves alone in places they shouldn't be alone, (like Bill Coveley) then you might be treated to one of Roger's rare pranks, or misdeeds as others would say.

Jolly Roger, it was claimed (although Roger, Sidney, or whatever alias he used bitterly refuted these claims) would chase a solitary child skipping, jumping, even pirouetting, (Bill Coveley claimed) until the child was cornered and Roger, the victor in this grotesque game of tiggy-tag would pinch him.

The pinch could be severe causing a blood blister, and a tirade of wailing sobs from the child. The victims, according to hearsay, would speak of Roger's eyes rolling back in his head as though the pinch itself had injected a stream of satisfaction which surged into him. Roger would smack his glossy crimson lips in ecstasy as though imbibing the feeling that his painful pinch to the child was giving him and would appear to be almost intoxicated by it.

Later, Roger would hand out pennies to the crying child saying he was sorry for hurting them and if they didn't tell their parents, he would reward them with a free ticket for all their friends and family next time the circus came to town. This was usually enough to buy the silence Roger wanted, but sometimes the children became sick afterwards, and no doctor could determine a reason for the sudden onset of gangrene and septicaemia that seemed to spread from a bruise on the child's arm, leg, or cheek. None of the children claimed they could remember how they came by the bruise of course. Before they could remember, they usually died.

Rumours spread; at the beginning mere tittle-tattle but it was enough to cause people to stay away from the sideshow and the rest of the circus. Eventually Sidney Erebus left the circus. Some said he was forced out by his performing family. He purchased a plot on Brightbell Pier where he paid for the construction of the 'Happy Fair Arcade' using money he had saved for such an entrepreneurial venture.

The Happy Fair Arcade was a place where most of the families from the town frequented. Frankie himself had played on most of the amusements within the arcade whenever his father had allowed him some free time, and when he had some pocket money to spend. The arcade had been there since the thirties, with Jolly Roger as its mascot throughout its time.

Sidney would manage the arcade and without his gaudy make-up he looked like any other middle-aged businessman. Occasionally, he would don the make-up and attire that had once made him famous and he would perform some of his balancing acts outside the arcade, drawing in the crowds once more, especially Frankie and his best friend Bill.

Bill and Frankie had gone to the Happy Fair Arcade to spend their pocket money. Frankie loved the mechanical machines and particularly the dancing automatons that resembled Jolly Roger himself. They had both watched the puppets dance and rode the carousel until they grew giddy. Eventually, the arcade started to empty as people began leaving for the allure of ice cream on the pier or shellfish on the promenade.

Bill had gone to the change booth to exchange a shilling for twelve pennies, so that he and Frankie could play on their favourite machine, where they would pull a pin to try and fire a marble into the clown's mouth and win a spearmint chewing gum stick. After a while Bill realised that nobody was operating the change booth, so he snuck inside to see if he could serve himself. Within moments, Jolly Roger had sprung up seemingly from nowhere. Startled, Bill ran back to Frankie. The pair of them were chased by Roger around the arcade and out onto the pier. Frankie, with his heart in his mouth ran as fast as his legs could carry him, which was quite fast, because Frankie was tall for his age, whereas Bill was a little undersized.

When Frankie came back looking for Bill, he found him sobbing, sitting cross-legged on the floor, his back up against the arcade. He was cradling his arm and said he wanted to go home. When Frankie asked what had happened, Bill just avoided the question, but eventually he simply said, 'Roger.'

As Frankie stood peering into the coppery vacant stare from within the open casket, he remembered the last time he had seen his friend Bill. He had called by to take some chocolate he had saved and to show him a model spitfire he had made using old pieces of wood, left over from some of his father's caskets.

Bill was laid out in bed and his arm looked bad. The skin was black and there was a rancid malodour about the room. His mother had daubed some yellow medicament on top that the doctor had given her and to Frankie it looked like mashed banana, but he knew it couldn't be.

Bill was looking frail, his eyes were yellowed, his lips blue. Frankie was only allowed to stay for a few brief moments, long enough to show Bill the spitfire. On seeing the aeroplane, he smiled weakly. Bill's mother later said it was the only time he'd smiled in weeks. Shortly after Frankie's visit Bill passed away.

Frankie assumed that Bill had told his parents what had happened at the arcade, because just before he had breathed his last breath, the police began to question Sidney after taking him into police custody. Sidney was threatened with imprisonment. The whole episode must have frightened him so much for after his temporary release (pending lack of evidence), he took a rope to his neck and hung himself off the end of Brightbell Pier. At least, that's what people said. A solitary early morning fisherman, who had gone out to take advantage of a high tide and an abandoned pier, found him suspended, twisting in the wind at the end of three yards of thick twine. Now Sidney/Roger was laid out before Frankie in his father's funeral parlour.

Since he'd been embalmed, few people had been to view the body. It seemed that Sidney had no living relatives of which to speak of. There had been a couple of curious busy bodies claiming to be old friends, and one unusual looking woman, an old sideshow friend who had laid a single rose on the lid of the casket before walking out whilst wiping away a tear on her heavily tattooed hand.

Frankie reached inside the casket. He intended to remove both coins from Sidney's eyes. After what he'd done to his friend Bill, he thought the ferryman could go without payment just this once. This stagnant, stiff cadaver didn't deserve a clear passage to the afterlife. The town was better off without him, Nirvana too.

As his fingers clasped around the coins he cried out in horror. He looked down to see that Roger's hand, (enclosed in a pristine white glove) had risen, his elbow was bent, and his fingers were squeezing the flesh of Frankie's arm, squeezing tightly in a pinch of death.

Frankie sat bolt upright. His bedroom was dark. He was panting and his heart was skipping beats as it throbbed against his sternum. His mouth dry, he flicked a switch on his bedside lamp. The shadows in his room withdrew slightly, and his breathing mellowed. It was the nightmare, the same nightmare he'd suffered every day since stealing the pennies from Roger's eyes. It had been almost a week since the casket had been taken from his father's funeral parlour and sent out to sea during hightide at Brightbell Sands, where Roger had been buried beneath the waves, according to his wishes.

Frankie glanced over to where he kept his tin clockwork moneybox. It was one of those humorous yet somewhat macabre moneyboxes where a skeletal hand once activated, emerged from underneath a small cloth shroud to drag a coin into a slot. The moneybox that had once been amusing now terrified him, because he imagined that he could hear the two large copper coins contained within, moving and flipping as he lay in his bed with his pillow folded around both ears to muffle the disconcerting noise.

He knew coins couldn't move by themselves and he tried to fool himself by dismissing the sounds as rats or some other nocturnal nuisance, possibly a beetle? When his own hoodwinking failed to provide the much-needed rest he craved he realised what he had to do, and he had to do it alone.

***

The night had tiptoed in fast as usual following the winter solstice. It was barely a quarter past four, and Frankie was jogging along the promenade towards Brightbell Pier holding a bicycle lamp, as thunder grumbled overhead and threatened an icy downpour.

He reached the pier and his legs devoured the distance along the board planks towards the Happy Fair Arcade.

As he passed by, the brisk wind had somehow managed to rattle the door open. It swung wide as if to entice him to take a look inside. Gusts rolled in off the sea and along the pier pushing against Frankie as he tried to step forwards into the salty spittle that was pitched at his frozen face.

He was getting soaked and his legs had almost given up the fight. He ducked into the dark doorway of the arcade, just for a minute or two he told himself, just until he got his breath, and the wind abated. Then it happened.

His hands were so numb with the wind chill and icy spray that he lost hold of one of the slippery coins he had been clutching so tightly. The penny dropped miraculously on its edge and rolled along the floor of the arcade away from him. He pointed his bicycle lamp and saw the coin roll out of sight and into the shadows.

Racing forwards he managed to keep the coin in his sights inside the loop of light cast from his lamp. He ran deeper inside the room, dashing past the assortment of bulky gaming machines; many of them stood to attention like silent soldiers, with one arm raised in a perpetual salute.

The coin came to rest against the feet of a red iron box. In the lamplight it resembled a short, squat, one-eyed robot from one of the many Hollywood science fiction movies he loved so much. He retrieved the coin and as he held it, he could hear the rain mixed with hail as it battered against the roof and the windows of the arcade. The storm outside had intensified.

Not wanting to brave the inclement weather outside and having lost the nerve to make his way alone along the final few feet to the end of the pier where Roger had dangled, he decided on a new course of action. He would push the coins into a machine within the arcade. The arcade was owned by Jolly Roger, and still had his name emblazoned across the front and around the walls inside. It was still part of him.

After the second coin dropped inside the red cast iron contrivance, he thought he could hear something, something distant. A sound like music faintly playing out from the machine. It sounded like circus music; a particular piece of music known as the 'galop'. The high tinny notes strained the thick air. Frankie didn't know the name of the composition slowly pouring into the space surrounding him, but he recognised the melody - it was the most recognisable popular form of circus music. A fast, lively tempo that was always used for daredevil acts, such as trick-riding or for trapeze artists.

Frankie backed away from the machine for he couldn't exit the arcade fast enough. He made his way through the rooms filled with mechanical gadgets, the lightning from outside scintillating and highlighting posters adorning the walls; posters of Jolly Roger grinning with wide red banana lips. Puppets and automatons quivered under his footfalls. He ran trying not to look at the things that looked back at him.

Once outside, he pulled the door shut and looked up to the heavens as the heavy droplets rained down washing his terrors away through the gaps in the boards of the pier, mixing with the churning tide below. He'd done it. He'd given the coins back to Roger and now his nightmares would surely stop. He hung his head as the wind pushed him back along the slippery wood towards the promenade.

David Ralph Williams lives in North Norfolk. He writes his ghost stories from an Edwardian farmhouse set deep in the Fens. He draws inspiration from his past as a ghost hunter and from the surrounding bleak, isolated landscape, often tinted by cold moonshine.

33055150R00120